A Chang

Looking for a new adve[...] a rubber tree. He is immedi[...]er rat, which bares a set of ra[...]his more timid brother, Kumal stands his ground. He moves slowly toward her and half closes his eyes in a killer look. He arches his back, lifts his head, and roars his little lungs out. The mother rat backs up a step, then scampers away with her young. Kumal does a bouncy victory dance. He has observed his father, and he is beginning to understand—tigers are the kings of the jungle.

He then spots Sangha above him, meowing in panic and climbing to a high branch of the rubber tree. Kumal meows for his brother to come down, but Sangha refuses to move. It's a long way down to the ground, and he is not about to risk it.

Kumal decides to climb up and rescue him. He scampers up to Sangha's rear end, catches his brother's tail in his teeth and proceeds to yank. When Sangha resists, Kumal pulls with all his strength. They hear an erratic banging echo in the distance, and the sound distracts them. Sangha loses his hold, and he and Kumal plunge to the cushy forest floor, unhurt but whimpering.

The two adult tigers have also heard the echo of the far-off noises, and to them the noises spell possible danger. The Great Tiger sits up, lets out a low growl and sniffs. At the same time the Tigress leaps to her feet.

A path cuts through the trees below, and a line of upright creatures makes it way through it. The Tigress bristles as she sees them. Although they are tall and thin and awkward beings, and appear to be harmless, she knows better. They are extremely dangerous.

TWO BROTHERS:
The Tale of Kumal and Sangha

A novel by James Ellison

Based on the motion picture screenplay written by
Alain Godard & Jean-Jacques Annaud

Newmarket Press • New York

This book is published in the United States of America.

First Edition

10 9 8 7 6 5 4 3 2 1

Library of Congress Cataloging-in-Publication Data

Ellison, James.
 Two brothers : the tale of Kumal and Sangha : a novel / by James Ellison ; based on the screenplay by Jean-Jacques Annaud and Alain Godard. — 1st ed.
   p. cm.
 ISBN 1-55704-632-8 (pbk. : alk. paper)
 1. Tigers—Juvenile fiction. [1. Tigers—Fiction.] I. Annaud, Jean-Jacques. II. Godard, Alain, screenwriter. III. Two brothers (Motion picture) IV. Title.
 PZ10.3.E5479Tw 2004
 [Fic]—dc22

                              2004026697

 ISBN 1-55704-632-8

QUANTITY PURCHASES

Companies, professional groups, clubs, and other organizations may qualify for special terms when ordering quantities of this title. For information, write Special Sales Department, Newmarket Press, 18 East 48th Street, New York, NY 10017; call (212) 832-3575; fax (212) 832-3629; or e-mail info@newmarketpress.com.

www.newmarketpress.com

Manufactured in the United States of America.

UNIVERSAL PICTURES AND PATHÉ PRESENT A PATHÉ RENN PRODUCTION/TWO BROTHERS PRODUCTIONS WITH TF1 FILMS PRODUCTION GUY PEARCE JEAN-CLAUDE DREYFUS FREDDIE HIGHMORE OANH NGUYEN PHILIPPINE LEROY BEAULIEU "TWO BROTHERS" MUSIC STEPHEN WARBECK COSTUME DESIGNER PIERRE-YVES GAYRAUD SUPERVISING SOUND EDITOR EDDY JOSEPH VISUAL EFFECTS FREDERIC MOREAU TIGERS TRAINED AND DIRECTED BY THIERRY LE PORTIER EDITING NOELLE BOISSON PRODUCTION DESIGNER PIERRE QUEFFELEAN DIRECTOR OF PHOTOGRAPHY JEAN-MARIE DREUJOU, AFC PRODUCER XAVIER CASTANO WRITTEN BY ALAIN GODARD & JEAN-JACQUES ANNAUD PRODUCER JAKE EBERTS PATHÉ! ÉCLAIR PG PARENTAL GUIDANCE SUGGESTED SOME MATERIAL MAY NOT BE SUITABLE FOR CHILDREN MILD VIOLENCE DTS PRODUCED AND DIRECTED BY JEAN-JACQUES ANNAUD SOUNDTRACK ON DECCA/UMG SOUNDTRACKS DOLBY DIGITAL A UNIVERSAL RELEASE UNIVERSAL © 2004 UNIVERSAL STUDIOS ⊕ For rating reasons, go to www.filmratings.com www.twobrothersmovie.net

To my children,
Owen and Brett,
animal lovers both

TWO BROTHERS

PART ONE

1

It is morning, deep in the Southeast Asian jungle, with not a breath of movement in the air. A symphony of sounds can be heard on the ground, in the trees, beneath the rocks and in the brush. A multi-colored hornbill takes flight from a bush wedged between two dislodged stones. He flies away, sounding the alarm with a deafening squawk. Alarms travel fast in the jungle—a panicked mongoose climbs onto the roots clinging to a stone wall overgrown with vegetation, then dives into a crevice.

The jungle is on the alert.

Branches crackle and a raspy breathing sound grows nearer as creatures on the receiving side of the wind smell danger and scatter. The brush shivers and sunlight filters through the branches, flashing on the surface of a wall, revealing the elegant remains of some bas-relief sculptures. The tangled vegetation is thrust aside and flattened. A male tiger advances. He ignores the moss-covered sculptures. They are not living creatures and pose no threat, nor do they offer the promise of food. They have been there—at one time well maintained and stunningly beautiful—through hundreds of generations of this animal's forebears.

The tiger suddenly whips through the air—a black and orange flash of movement. He leaps and breaks the silence with a savage roar. A shadow of a great female tiger is splayed against the rock face, and she slides stealthily along the bas-relief sculptures, which depict a line of elephants, all outfitted for a hunt. The hunters astride the elephants' backs are armed with lances pointed toward their prey: a tiger poised to pounce.

A defiant growl rings out, followed by a massive roar. The great tiger is panting. He can smell the tigress now and his greenish-golden eyes glow with intensity. He is perfectly still, keenly expectant, as he scans the curtain of jungle before him. His nostrils quiver and taste the air. He moves slowly, one paw, then another, over the loose tiles of a terrace that overlooks the sculptures. His ears flatten to his head, he growls again— *"Grrrrrrrrr"*— in a kind of question. He is searching for the source of the smell.

Directly in front of him, a few hundred paces away, the ferns shiver. Again the tiger is still, save for his head, which turns to the source of the movement and sound. Through the ferns emerges a female tiger. Her smell intoxicates the great tiger. The two of them face off, as still as the air that clings moistly to the jungle earth. They regard each other as though mesmerized. Only their twitching tails move.

The female tiger's muscles suddenly relax. As if in slow motion, she lies down on the mossy floor, emitting a faint guttural sound. With a languid stretch, she then rolls slowly onto her side, licks a paw, and arches her back. Her eyes are locked on the great tiger's.

He answers the invitation with a deep growl as he bounds toward her. She springs up and disappears into the ferns and dashes into the dark green shadow of the huge trees that shut out the sky. Her ocher coat flashes over the collapsed ramparts covered with jasmine vines and moist orchids as she rushes in through an opening under a vaulted rock wall. The great tiger, hot in pursuit of her, follows her inside.

The mating dance is on.

The tigress approaches a pile of collapsed chiseled blocks, causing a group of frightened howling monkeys to scramble to safety at the top of a giant tree, whose ghostly roots wrap around the broken remains of a majestic portal. The massive tentacles of the tree appear to hold in their grasp blocks of stone, pushing them upward as an offering to the sky. At the foot of the octopus tree, two sandstone Buddha statues guard a dark entryway partially hidden by a curtain of vines.

The tigress storms inside and just as quickly comes out again with the great tiger close on her heels. Food is forgotten; danger is ignored: every nerve and fiber of the big cat's being is now concentrated on the tigress. The great tiger and the tigress roll around on the spongy ground, mixing low guttural growls. They rear up and slap at each other, then hug each other, then fend each other off in a duet of ferocious growls, their eyes locked together. The mating dance continues as the tigress flees down the gallery of a dilapidated cloister, bounding gracefully from stone to stone, aware of her pursuer pounding along behind her. Poised atop the remains of a shattered sculpture, she leaps up onto a carved pedestal and stretches out, waiting.

The bats hanging upside down from the ceiling begin to rustle uneasily. They are on their guard, aware of danger and ready for flight. When they see the great tiger approaching, their furry bodies spread their bald membranes. As though a signal has passed among them, the swarm of bats takes flight in a concert of piercing shrieks, rushing through the vines between the two Buddhas guarding the entrance. With a furious flapping of black wings, they fly up to the dome atop the vast sea of vegetation. A short distance beyond where they alight, four towers emerge from the overgrown temple.

From that vantage point, the bats watch as the mating dance is drawing to a close. The echo of the tigers' passionate coupling ricochets through the vaulted galleries and reaches the remote corners of the buried temple. The sound rolls through the galleries where a line of benevolent Buddhas slumbers under a thick layer of dust. The sound echoes through an alcove where a colossal sandstone Vishnu—a drop of moisture trickling down the moss-green crack on his cheek like a tear running down a scar—stands in the shadow, wearing vestments of dripping vines. The echo of their mating reverberates alongside a procession of smiling, dancing girls carved in the stone wall, and reaches into every niche and cranny where disciples sit in profound meditation.

The jungle is momentarily taken over, consumed, by the roar of the tigers, which seems to awaken the countless forgotten treasures from their centuries-long sleep.

Most living creatures, however, listen intently and remain silent.

2

The year is 1923, and in one of London's largest auction houses two clerks stagger under the weight of a pair of heavy elephant tusks, which they carry onto the auctioneer's platform. "Five hundred guineas," says the auctioneer with a fond glance at the beautiful curved ivory. He pauses for a moment and scans the room, waiting for a response. "Come now, ladies and gentlemen," he says, "who will start at five hundred guineas for this magnificent pair of tusks? I have never seen finer…"

Although all of London's major collectors are gathered in the room, no one is bidding. The auctioneer's voice rises a note in supplication. "Please, ladies and gentlemen…This ivory is exceptional, absolutely first-rate. As you know, these tusks are being offered for sale by Mr. Aidan McRory himself, which guarantees their museum quality."

There are still no bids. Despite the auctioneer's practiced enthusiasm, the distinguished audience remains stonily indifferent. The bane of any auctioneer's existence is to establish an opening bid level which he then has to lower, but the unhappy auctioneer has no choice.

"Very well," he says. "Four hundred fifty guineas. Do I hear four hundred fifty guineas for these priceless tusks?"

When there are still no bids, the auctioneer glances helplessly toward the rear of the room where Aidan McRory stands aloof against the wooden paneling, his expression impossible to read—perhaps world-weary, perhaps stoic, perhaps something half-formed and buried deep within his secretive nature. The auctioneer's dilemma appears to leave him cold; McRory seems indifferent in the face of the disaster unfolding on the auctioneer's platform.

A stylish woman has followed the auctioneer's imploring glance. What she sees makes an instant impression on her: a slender, deeply tanned man in his thirties, with lean, handsome features and the athletic build of a born adventurer. She has seen his face on the jackets of his books.

She turns to her companion and leans close to her. "Look who's standing at the back. None other than Aidan McRory."

"Yes, it's McRory all right," her companion says, nodding. "I always adore the way he looks…England's great white hunter. Have you ever read James Oliver Curwood, the American naturalist?"

"No."

"McRory reminds me of Curwood's hunters. Smart, brave—marching to the sound of their own drummer." The companion smiles. "Maybe even a bit dangerous."

"You know him, don't you?"

"Not well. We've attended some of the same parties."

"Introduce me to him—*please*. I want to live danger-ously."

"Not *that* dangerously, my dear. He has a reputation of being very difficult, and besides, it's not the right moment. His poor tusks have been neglected. He isn't having a very good morning."

"I still want to meet him." She smiles into her velvet glove. "Poor man and his big old tusks. I could cheer him up."

On the platform the clerks sag under the weight of the tusks and sweat profusely. The auctioneer's voice takes on a strained note of desperation. "We're going to bid at three hundred guineas," he says. "At three hun-dred these tusks are an absolute steal."

In the back, McRory shifts his weight just perceptibly forward onto the balls of his feet. He has seen enough. Discreetly—no more than the lifting of the first finger of his right hand—he signals for the bidding to close. The clerks lower their burden to the floor with audible relief, and the auctioneer, feeling relief of his own, announces the next lot.

"With the next offering, ladies and gentlemen," he says, recapturing his earlier enthusiasm, "we leave Africa and journey halfway across the globe to Southeast Asia. A thirteenth-century sandstone Buddha from the unex-plored reaches of the Upper Mekong region, this is a very rare piece indeed. I'll start the bidding at two thousand guineas."

McRory slowly makes his way toward the exit, but pauses when he hears a murmur of admiration and excitement ripple through the room. He listens as the auctioneer says, "Two thousand five hundred guineas on my left. Do I hear three thousand? Three thousand in front...Three thousand five hundred on my right." McRory turns and stares intently at the pinkish sand statue of a Buddha smiling mysteriously in its place of honor on the platform. He feels that there is no way that statue can compare with his beautiful ivory tusks, but it's clear that the audience does not share his enthusiasm for ivory. He watches as a blue titmouse adorning the red hat of a dowager in the first row gives a small nod.

"Four thousand," the auctioneer says, perspiration glistening on his forehead.

A heavy-featured Indian Army Colonel with a thick, pointy mustache raises a pen in the air.

"Forty-five hundred on my right. Five thousand—five thousand—do I hear five thousand?"

The monocle of a cold-eyed London banker drops softly to the end of its cord.

"Five thousand," the auctioneer says, quickening his pace. He is having trouble keeping up with the onslaught of bids.

"Six thousand on the left," he says.

"Seven thousand in the back of the room."

"Eight thousand…"

"Nine thousand…"

McRory observes the fast mounting bidding with frank astonishment. It is painfully obvious to him that British high society has set aside its usual reserve and has grown feverishly and openly acquisitive—but why? And for what? He wonders how there can be such frenzy over these rather dim artifacts. He has no idea why, but he knows that he had better come up with some answers. Has ivory suddenly lost its charm?

The auctioneer's gavel finally comes down with a firm thump. "Eleven thousand guineas. Congratulations to the gentleman in the third row."

Loud applause greets the end of the bidding. McRory shakes his head, and the only outward sign of the incredulity he's feeling is a slightly raised eyebrow. He approaches the next lot, which the clerks are placing at the base of the platform, and takes a long look at the ancient statues—some of them chipped and bruised, all of them worn—waiting to capture the collectors' fancy. McRory looks thoughtful as he studies the statues.

3

The sun rises red as blood across the breadth of the jungle. The fiercely beautiful light shines on the sugar-loaf towers of a buried temple and highlights the glints of gold that covered them in splendor many centuries ago. A toothless Macaque monkey is perched on the highest branch of a Banyan tree and lets out a cry of alarm that skips over the treetops. A deer buck straight-ens up, on his guard at the end of a terrace, his flanks shivering. He scans the piles of collapsed stone terraces, porticos strangled by vines, stairways overgrown with ferns, and lets loose a short cry, which is relayed from den to lair, from burrow to perch, in a medley of differ-ent voices.

The cries all carry the same message: beware of dan-ger. Something is out there, carried on the wind. The monkeys scatter into the foliage and there is general panic on the ground. Wild boar gallop away, a herd of gazelle skips quickly from bush to bush, and at the foot of a broken statue, hyenas and vultures abandon a car-cass swarming with flies.

By the stone staircase leading up to the buried tem-ple, a tiger cub, Kumal, appears. Flanked by two stone Buddhas, he watches with wide-eyed satisfaction as the lesser creatures of the jungle take off running. He is only a cub, born three weeks earlier, but he already senses his power. Another tiger cub, his brother Sangha, joins him, along with their mother, the Tigress.

A mighty roar is heard from afar. The Tigress raises her head and responds: *"Ah-oom! Ah-oom!"*

On the deserted banks, the Great Tiger waits, sniffing the air. White water rushes over rocks and spills into a calm pool surrounded by wild banana and coconut trees.

"Ah-oom!" he roars out again to his mate.

The Tigress appears through a green wall of lush growth and the male takes several steps toward her. He growls softly as he rubs his head against the fragrant neck of his mate.

Kumal and Sangha move under him and rub their sides against their father's legs. They are in a playful mood, cuffing each other and doing miniature growl imitations of their parents. The Great Tiger approves of their play and rewards them with a few powerful licks to their faces and flanks. They respond to his ministrations by washing him with their tiny pink tongues.

Kumal jumps over his brother and Sangha does the same in turn. With high spirits and a lot of chatter, they continue to play leapfrog and roll around on the ground and rear up on their hind legs to fight like two baby gladiators. Kumal drops his tail under Sangha's snout. Sangha grabs it and Kumal drags him toward the river. Sangha hangs on like a water-skier and leaves tracks in the sand of the riverbank behind him. As they frolic, their parents lie side by side watching their children chase and splash each other in the water.

Sangha climbs up on a stone carved into squares while Kumal scurries onto an engraved rock. Near the temple even the riverbed has been carved with sacred figures. The cubs lie together panting from their exertions—but only for a moment. There is so much to explore in this brand-new world of theirs—shapes and sizes and smells and sounds—and with their unlimited energy they cannot remain still for long. Kumal dips his thick paw into the clear water, feeling around the bottom for the giant frog carved in the stone. And Sangha, sitting on top of another stone, seems perplexed as he starts sliding along the surface of the water. He is not sitting on a stone at all, as he discovers to his amazement, but on the back of a tortoise moving toward the shore. Hunched on top of his armored vehicle, Sangha disappears into the thicket. With a cry, Kumal takes off after his brother and the curious stone that moves.

As the blazing sun rises higher in the cobalt sky, the two brothers roll around together on the mossy ground. In their play they come across a small coconut—their first coconut as almost everything for them right now is their very first experience. They push it back and forth, catch it on the bounce and grab it between their paws like kittens playing with a ball of wool. When the coconut eludes their grasp and rolls down a steep hillside, the two happy cubs tumble down after it, falling head over heels.

Keeping a close eye on their children, the Great Tiger and the Tigress are taking a peaceful dip in the warm water. The Tigress rests her head on the Great Tiger's broad back and purrs deep in her throat. But even then, at her most relaxed, she is on guard, listening to the far-off sounds of her twin children's games and prepared to spring into action at the slightest provocation.

A small rodent is rousted from its hiding place and bolts through Sangha's legs. Trailing the little critter to the foot of a rubber tree, Sangha finds himself nose to nose with the small rodent's mother. He stops in his tracks, as confused by her as he was by the moving stone. The large mother rat spits angrily at the tiger cub and he backs away in panic, the hair on his back rising. The rodent spits again, and that is enough for Sangha, who turns tail and beats a quick retreat.

At the bottom of the hill, Kumal has lost interest in the furry coconut ball and, looking for a new adventure, trots toward the rubber tree. He is immediately confronted by the mother rat, who hisses and bares a set of razor-sharp teeth. But unlike his more timid brother, Kumal stands his ground. He moves slowly toward her and half closes his eyes in a killer look, not learned but bred in the bone. He arches his back, lifts his head and roars his little lungs out. The mother rat now has second thoughts and backs up a step, then scampers away with her young and disappears down a hole. Kumal does a bouncy victory dance, running around and around the rubber tree. He has observed his father and now he is beginning to understand—tigers are the kings of the jungle. Ecstatic, he climbs up on a rock and lets out another mighty roar, louder than the last one, and rolls over on his back.

He then spots Sangha above him, meowing in panic and climbing to a high branch of the rubber tree, which is oozing a mess of milky white sap. Kumal stands at the base of the tree, his paws on the bark, and meows for his brother to come down. But Sangha is frozen with fear and indecision and refuses to move. His claws dig deep into the rubber tree, lacerating the bark. From Sangha's perspective it's a long way down to the ground and he is not about to risk it.

Kumal decides to climb up and rescue him. He scampers up to Sangha's rear end, catches his brother's tail in his teeth and proceeds to yank. When Sangha resists, Kumal pulls in the opposite direction with all his strength while hanging onto his brother's tail in midair. They hear an erratic banging echo in the distance, carried on the breeze from the valley, and the sound distracts them. Sangha loses his hold, and he and Kumal plunge onto the cushy forest floor, unhurt but whimpering.

* * *

The two adult tigers have also heard the echo of the far-off noises, and, to them, the noises spell possible danger. The Great Tiger sits up, lets out a low growl and sniffs. At the same time the Tigress leaps to her feet and dashes off in the direction she saw her little ones go. She runs low to the ground—a graceful blur of motion.

Kumal carefully approaches a bluff halfway up the hillside; his head fits neatly through a round opening in the leaves. Sangha, covered with the rubber tree's sap, trails behind him, waddling along like a duck. Large rubber tree leaves are stuck to his feet, and he looks as though he's plodding through mud wearing snowshoes.

The banging from far off continues. Kumal tilts his head in the direction of the sound, wondering what it can be. In his imagination he conjures up the image of a soft-edged oval shape, a shape he had seen in the first week of his life, and a woodpecker hammering against a hollow tree trunk. Sangha's more apprehensive imagination summons up a very different picture from his brother's. Inside the soft-edged oval appears a Macaque monkey banging a coconut against a rock and baring its teeth in a snarl. Each blow the monkey makes is in perfect rhythm with the far-off banging.

On the bluff, Kumal and Sangha take another step forward. From the clearing they have an open view of the valley. A path cuts through the trees below, and a line of upright creatures makes its way through it. The Tigress bristles as she sees them. She has a memory of them from when she was a cub, and although they are tall and thin and awkward beings, and appear to be

harmless, she knows better. They are extremely dangerous and have their own special ways to kill.

She springs from the thicket and growls menacingly,
from low in her throat. *"Rarrr....Rarrr!"*

Sangha, tangled up in thorns and unable to extricate
himself, mews desperately. His mother grabs him in her
teeth and hurries back up toward the bluff. She enters a
hidden den inside a vine-infested chapel and puts
Sangha down. A moment later Kumal comes trotting
up. The mother gives her boisterous son a light cuff on
the snout. She then lies down on the soft moss and
begins licking away the rubbery substance still stuck on
Sangha's paws. Once she finishes cleaning his paws, the
Tigress rolls over on her side and nurses her young.

The long day in the Upper Mekong is drawing to a
close and shadows of dusk stretch toward the ruined
terraces. With the fading of the light, the creatures that
inhabit the night begin singing their songs. The Great
Tiger leaps into position outside the temple and
remains there, concealed, a vigilant sentry. His tail
snaps in the air and his nostrils quiver as he inventories
the various smells that surround him in order to isolate
those that spell trouble. He utters a low growl at the
echo of the sounds growing closer.

Night falls with a profound depth of blackness.
Sangha is fast asleep, snoring softly, cuddled against his
mother's warm belly. Kumal, however, is too curious to
sleep. His brand new world is alive with amazing dis-
coveries. He climbs along a root and stretches up to a

crack in the wall of the chapel and looks out to the tiled courtyard, which glimmers with a strange light. To the Tigress, the light is more ominous than strange. She lies very still, ready to pounce, to flee—to do whatever is necessary to protect her young. She listens to the strange music coming from outside somewhere. Danger is palpable in the air.

4

The upright creatures have stopped for the night and they are hanging large nets between the trees. Some of these curious, sticklike creatures with their hairless bodies are already lying inside the nets, asleep. Others build a fire in the temple's central tiled courtyard.

Kumal's attention fixes on the pale-skinned upright creature in white. He is seated near the fire smoking a pipe. The man, Aidan McRory, suddenly stops writing and looks up from his bound notebook. He scans the landscape around him, wrapped now in darkness, as he draws deeply on his pipe. After a moment, he puts a record on the phonograph next to him. The sounds of Verdi fill the tiled courtyard of the ruined temple and float softly on the night air. As the music reaches a crescendo and then fades to a somber, dying fall, McRory rises and takes a few steps toward a mural, which depicts graceful Apsaras carved in the stone and dancing in the flickering light of the fire. McRory contemplates the mural as he puffs on his pipe. He parts the hanging vines and gently strokes the grain of the sandstone face.

Watching this pale upright creature and listening to the unaccustomed sounds coming from near him,

Kumal's ears begin to vibrate. Through the crack, the little tiger looks with surprise at the rectangular box upon which a big tulip arises, the source of the melodious sounds. As he continues to listen, other, less melodious sounds capture his attention. He stretches out his neck and sees a servile dog yelping and groveling at the heels of his master, wagging his tail and begging for his bone.

Kumal emits a low growl. Instinctively, he does not like the dog, but the haunting music continues to sing in his head.

* * *

Hours later, the early morning sun filters through the leaves, devouring the cool air of night. It seems to awaken a colossal Buddha and he smiles benevolently at the new day. What the Buddha does not know is that a stick of explosive has been inserted in a crack of the pedestal that supports his mammoth feet. McRory returns the Buddha's smile and gives a jaunty salute with the first two fingers of his right hand. He then brings the burning bowl of his pipe to the fuse of the stick of dynamite, and steps back.

At the very moment McRory lights the fuse, which will end seven centuries of the Buddha's reign over his designated spot of jungle earth, Kumal and Sangha are sleeping in each other's arms, cuddled against their mother's warm coat, their tiny pink bellies rising and falling in unison. Sangha has his brother's ear in his mouth and he suckles it in his sleep.

The loud explosion reverberates through the jungle. The Tigress bolts upright, and her head moves back and forth like a periscope. She watches the dust and blue smoke rising from the collapsed Buddha, her head cocked to one side. She watches the pale upright creature, a smoking curved stick stuck in his mouth, walk over to the fallen Buddha and stare down at it. He smiles, then begins scratching at the lichen and gangue covering its shoulders.

In the temple courtyard, workers have begun their tasks. A group armed with machetes dislodges the pink sandstone statues from the tangle of vegetation that imprisons them. They uproot them from their alcoves with crowbars, causing them to fall to the ground. Another group extricates the bas-reliefs as the plaques break. Nearby, still another group is clearing the vines that strangle an enormous sandstone idol.

The Tigress watches, her golden eyes gleaming in the sun.

Another creature wearing a shapeless hat joins the pale upright creature with the smoking stick. "Big money," he says to McRory, the hunter. "But too big to carry. What do we do? We take the head only?"

McRory studies the massive statue in silence, survivor of so many centuries and with beauty undiminished by time. Finally he nods and says, "Yes, Napoleon, take the head. That's the best we can do."

The workers start decapitating the idol with sledge-hammers and chisels. Using his trunk as a hoist, an elephant helps the men load the booty onto wagons pulled by water buffalo. In the middle of the courtyard, the cook teases the fire under a kettle. Branches are crackling, and a breeze blows the smoke toward the ruins where the tigers are hiding. The capricious breeze suddenly shifts direction, blowing the smoke back in the cook's face, and he walks around to the other side of the fire, coughing. Seated at the feet of Napoleon, a dog sniffs the air now coming from the direction of the temple, a message written clearly on the wind. The dog bristles, leaps up and bares his fangs. The elephant trumpets. The water buffalo, too, are aroused from their lethargy by the message in the air. They strain against their ropes in panic.

"Tiger," Napoleon cries out. "There's a tiger out there."

Unseen and still as the Buddha, the Tigress continues to watch them with her golden eyes.

* * *

The Great Tiger rises. He jumps down onto a stone console and slips silently through the roots that hide the temple entrance. His eyes take in the scene before him and his nose gauges the wind. He moves with the utmost stealth, knowing that he is close to the danger line where the wind is split and can blow in any direction.

The pale upright creature stands in the paved courtyard and waves his arms.

"Verlaine," he calls out. "The rifle. Be quick about it."

As a worker comes running over with a Winchester, McRory turns to Napoleon and says, "Take yours, too. Let's move out."

On top of a root, inquisitive Kumal peeks through the crack in the wall, while nearby, through a small opening in the columns, the Tigress observes men running and carrying rifles. She can also see that a dog is leading them toward the temple entrance. Silently, the Tigress drops down to the chapel floor. She swings around swiftly as Sangha rushes to her side, trembling with fear, another rubber leaf now stuck to his paw. Noiselessly she reaches out a paw and grabs him by the scruff of the neck. Holding him, she leaps up to a ledge and disappears inside a dark tunnel at the top of the vault. Left alone, but too busy to be concerned, Kumal comes down off his perch. But his brother and mother are nowhere to be seen. He looks at the tunnel through which his mother fled, and a new emotion, fear, enters his being for the first time. He meows. He whimpers. His small body shivers.

Aidan McRory enters the temple, his rifle cocked, and Napoleon follows close behind him, his rifle also at the ready. The dog sniffs at the stone tiles and whines as he picks up on the pungent, acidic scent of the wildcats.

With his tail between his hind legs, he sticks close to his master, still whining and barely able to contain himself.

McRory proceeds slowly into the darkness of the temple's interior, pointing his rifle, left, right, and straight ahead. The two men come up to the statue of the weeping Vishnu, and ahead two galleries open out on each side of the pedestal. McRory hesitates, then nods to Napoleon to take the left passage. He takes the right, and moves forward, a slow, cautious step at a time.

From deep inside the den, Kumal hears the men's footsteps and he can smell them. It is a new smell to him, as most everything is new, and it frightens him. He tries to make himself invisible as a shadow grows larger and larger on the wall. The silhouette of Napoleon appears at the opening of the gallery. He's heading straight for the chapel and he has spotted the tiger cub. Growling, Kumal retreats and winds up back at the wall and tries once more to leap onto the ledge. As Napoleon advances and has the cub in his rifle sights, a bone-chilling roar fills the ruins like a bomb blast, and the Great Tiger leaps out from behind the rock pile. In a second he is swarming all over Napoleon, pins him to the ground and plants his claws into the flesh of his shoulders. Kumal watches his father, still shivering with fright, but he is also beginning to feel the first vestiges of a new and swelling emotion. What his father is doing is not play, as he and Sangha and his mother have played. This is different, this is real and meant to hurt and destroy, and the force of this new insight thrills Kumal and sends blood in hot streams through his body. He adds his small snarls to his father's loud, raw snarls.

Suddenly Kumal sees another upright shadow growing larger and larger on the wall and he can smell the faintest whiff of smoke. McRory is now standing in plain sight pointing his rifle at the Great Tiger. Kumal watches his every move. He hears a click and then sees a flash of light accompanied by a popping sound. Kumal watches as the Great Tiger, his father, collapses to the ground, hiding Kumal. Hearing the shot, the workers rush into the gallery toward the ruined chapel. McRory leans over Napoleon and examines his injured arm.

"You'll live," he says. "It's superficial. Luckily the cat didn't have time to do much damage."

"It hurts like hell," Napoleon says as he grits his teeth and rolls his eyes in pain.

"We'll patch you up and you'll be fine in no time."

Napoleon nods. "I'm surprised he didn't go for my throat."

"You never know with animals. They're as unpredictable as we are." He pulls out his handkerchief and expertly fashions a tourniquet. "What's the bounty for a tiger in these parts?"

"Two hundred fifty piastres."

"Not bad," McRory says. "I'll see that you get the money." He grins. "Payment for your battle wounds. You've earned it, my friend."

Kumal, in the meantime, squats, belly to ground, trembling in the dark. He curls into a tight knot, trying to hide from these terrifying upright creatures. They speak some strange language, and they smell of smoke and meat.

"All right," the pale upright creature says to other creatures now gathered in the den, "you two get the front legs. You two lift the hind legs. Bloody heavy, isn't he? All right—let's go! One, two, three!"

Kumal can feel the mass above him begin to move. Light flows in from above as the workers lift the carcass of the Great Tiger, revealing the tiger cub hiding underneath. Now exposed, Kumal has no choice but to confront these creatures like a real tiger. Imitating the behavior of his father earlier, he snarls as McRory raises his rifle. Cub and man make eye contact, and slowly the man points the rifle to the ground.

Napoleon stares at him, his forehead wrinkled in surprise. "What's the matter, boss?" he says. "A tiger cub grows into a tiger, you know. And when he does, he will kill you as soon as look at you. You're a hunter. Hunters don't have soft hearts."

McRory grins at his helper and shrugs off his remarks. "This little guy will make a good sweetener for the chief—a splendid gift. I need the old boy on my side."

Kumal watches the pale white creature warily as he comes close. Trying what worked with the mother rat, he puffs himself up and lets out a fearsome growl, showing his claws and baring his ferocious baby teeth. But this pale upright creature is no mother rat. He shows no fear. He smiles and comes ever closer.

5

Still holding Sangha in her teeth, the Tigress flees through the brush and tall grass and doesn't slow down until she reaches the top of a hill. Below her, Verlaine scans the tall grass swaying in the breeze, but the feline has eluded him. A short time later the workers give up the search.

The Tigress and Sangha lie together in the tall grass and occasionally the feline cries out. She is crying to the Great Tiger, she is crying out to her intrepid son Kumal. Her long muscular body shudders with grief, and her timid son, close up beside her, feels the movement of her grief and burrows more deeply into his mother's warmth. Nestled there, he never wants to leave her side.

* * *

As the wagon travels along an ancient road in the jungle, McRory sits on the front of the wagon, which is overflowing with bas-reliefs. He holds the cub firmly as it snarls and struggles mightily to be released. Kumal scratches, he bites, he howls. He is furious at this strange new restraint on his movements and overpowered by the smell of smoke that emanates from this pale upright creature. He is desperate to find a way to escape those white hands with strange slender fingers that imprison him.

"My, aren't you the ferocious one," McRory says. "But you know what I think? It's my considered opinion that you are bluffing, little fellow. I think your bark is far worse than your bite." He holds the cub tight against his body as he talks to him softly. "You'll tire out before I do, you know. So you might as well relax and enjoy the ride."

The hunter talks steadily to the baby tiger as the caravan travels over the rut-filled road that winds through the heart of the jungle. Kumal continues to struggle in the man's arms, but as the hours pass and the cub grows accustomed to this new voice speaking softly in his ear he begins to relax.

The workers bend under the weight of the precious finds torn from the temple. Piled into the wagons, balanced on bamboo poles, tied to palanquins, and laden on the back of the elephant are the smiling divinities, graceful Apsaras and meditating wise men—all cruelly wrenched from their once-forgotten redoubt. Beside these sandstone pieces are the remains of the Great Tiger, hung up by the paws on a length of bamboo. Hanging in more or less the same position, with his wounded arm raised, Napoleon brings up the rear.

The caravan comes to an ancient bridge where eighteen Buddha statues eternally guard the approach. The water buffalo pause to drink from a murky stream, and the elephant sprays itself, creating a miniature geyser. The workers break open coconuts and tip them up to quench their thirst.

"Hold him for me, will you?" McRory says, handing Kumal to Verlaine. Cautiously, the worker grasps the tiger cub by the scruff of the neck, while Kumal, removed from the arms of the man of smoke with the soft voice, once again twists and wriggles furiously. Sensing that this upright creature is not as gentle as the one who held him before, Kumal intensifies his struggle and tries to bite through the skin of his forearm.

McRory removes a tin of honey drops from his hunting bag, places one in his mouth and dissolves several others in the water in his canteen. He then takes Kumal back, immobilizes the tiger cub under his left arm, and brings the canteen to his mouth.

"Now cheer up, little chap," McRory says as he rubs the cub under his chin. "There's no way you can fight me, so enjoy yourself. Everything is going to be spot on."

After the short rest stop, the caravan continues on its way through the jungle. Intense heat filters down through the trees and causes the air to ripple with countless mirages. At the front of the wagon, Kumal's head begins to nod, and little by little, nestled in McRory's arms, his eyes close. The hammering of the buffalo hooves on the roadway become soft background music to him—a distant sound that grows ever fainter as sleep comes closer. The tiger cub sucks the last sweet-tasting drops from the canteen as McRory absentmind-edly strokes his white belly.

"Enough now, you greedy little bugger," McRory says. "It's empty. You've sucked it dry."

Kumal half opens an eye and watches sleepily as the canteen is taken away from him. Without thinking, he grasps the finger within his reach and begins sucking on it instead. The sucking comforts him, as does the bodily warmth of the pale upright creature with his smoky smell. McRory watches the cub sucking on his finger and, after a brief hesitation, decides to leave it there. The poor little fellow just lost his father, he thinks, and he's separated from his mother—not exactly a pretty picture for him. The least I can do is lend the little bloke my finger.

"He won't get that kind of treatment from the chief," Verlaine says. "He has mean ways."

"Is that so?" McRory gives an extra nudge to the cub's belly. "Well, maybe I won't give him to the chief then. Maybe I'll keep him for myself."

Something in the man's tone reaches deep inside Kumal, and he looks up and meets McRory's eyes. The eyes, blue like a pale morning sky, no longer threaten him. Instead, they slow his heart rate and fill him with a sense of peace. After a moment, rocked by the jolts of the road, little by little, his eyelids close once more. His head resting against the butt of the rifle, he starts purring softly in the warmth of the pale upright man.

A moment later McRory feels something warm and wet, and looks down. A dark stain spreads on his trousers under the pink belly of the tiger cub. McRory shakes his head and a slow grin spreads across his features. "Why you just make yourself at home, little fellow." McRory wants to shift his leg and look for a dry cloth to wipe his pants, but as he looks down at the tiger cub sleeping peacefully in the warmth of his lap, he doesn't have the heart to wake him from his contented slumber. *I shot your father*, McRory thinks with a sudden stab of sadness. *I owe you something.*

After a brief hesitation, he removes the scarf from around his neck and with the greatest delicacy diapers the baby tiger's bottom with it.

6

The sun has now risen into the center of the sky. In the rice paddies, villagers tending the fields call out to one another. They drop their tools and hurry toward the convoy of wagons coming out of the forest. With the canopy of the jungle now behind them, the sun pounds down on the wagon in which Kumal is sleeping. He slowly opens his eyes and sees men running; they crowd around the remains of the Great Tiger and shout joyfully. Clapping hands and singing, the villagers celebrate the great white hunter, Aidan McRory, and they form an honor guard for the convoy as it enters the village of straw huts built on piles.

The newness of the world continues to assault Kumal with its many sights and sounds and smells, a dizzying blend of mysterious elements, which he is only beginning to comprehend and sort out. He sniffs McRory's pocket, grasps it and tries to put his paw inside. The white man, with a shrug, finally gives in. He removes from his pocket the box decorated with bees and hives and surrenders it to Kumal. The tiger cub, tied with a rope to the leg of the small stool on which McRory sits, rolls the fragrant box around and around as he did with the furry coconut ball. As Kumal nudges the box back and forth with his nose and issues a series of soft meows, McRory is engaged in delicate negotiations with an Annamese man wearing a French beret on which a number of medals are pinned. They are sitting on the veranda of a straw hut mounted on stilts. A young female draped in a simple cotton sarong that leaves her shoulders bare speaks to McRory from some distance away. With a nearly flawless English accent, she says, "My father, the chief, thanks you in the name of our village. He thanks you most gratefully for killing the tiger. We are indeed much safer because of you."

McRory nods but says nothing, sensing that she isn't finished. He is struck favorably by her sultry good looks and her soft, melodious voice; she gives every indication of good breeding and high intelligence. She looks down and checks the pages of an old exercise book to find the exact words she is looking for. Staring directly into McRory's eyes for the first time, she says, "The tiger brings death, death and destruction, to our people. They kill our buffalo, our chickens, and too often the citizens of our village. We truly honor you, Mr. McRory, for the death of our enemy."

The young woman stands in the shadows and McRory leans forward, straining to get a better look at her.

"What is your name?" he asks.

After a slight hesitation, she says, "Nai-Rea."

"Well, Nai-Rea, tell the chief—your father—tell him I'm glad to have been of service in return for the help he has given me. Next year, if I return for more statues,

I will need his assistance again. In the meantime, I know I can count on his friendship and his discretion."

The chief, listening with only minimal comprehension and nodding vigorously, breaks into a big smile of blackened teeth. He spits out a long line of red juice from his betel chew and responds in his native language. McRory wears a look of great concentration, but understands virtually nothing of what is said. When the chief finishes his speech, Nai-Rea translates. "The chief says that discretion is the Oriental's virtue."

McRory smiles, hoping for an answering light in her eyes. "It seems as though he said much more than that."

Nai-Rea's answering smile is patient and fleeting. "That was essentially the message."

Kumal pushes the tin of honey drops and it strikes the bottom of the stool, forcing the lid open. The little tiger leaps out to the length of the restraining rope in pursuit of the honey drops as they spill onto the floor. Ignoring the cub's antics, McRory says, "I would like to thank your father, the chief, for all that he has done. Please tell him that I will give him the hide as a sign of my gratitude."

He shifts his position on the stool and squints his eyes in another attempt to get a clearer view of the young woman's face.

The chief mumbles something to his daughter in response to her translation, and she says, "The chief appreciates your great generosity, but he would rather have him alive."

"Alive?" McRory looks at her with a raised eyebrow. "I'm not clear exactly what you mean. He's dead. This is his hide."

The chief points a thick dark finger at the tiger cub busily crunching on a honey drop with little purrs of delight. He recognizes the taste of the enchanting drink from the canteen.

McRory shakes his head. "I'm afraid there's a misunderstanding, Nai-Rea. I'm offering the chief the big tiger, the dead one. Not the cub. I plan to keep the cub."

The girl nods solemnly, translates for her father, and then listens to his agitated, rapid-fire response.

"The chief says the dead one is most welcome," she translates for McRory, "and his gratitude knows no bounds. He wants to assure you that he is delighted to receive both tigers."

"I see. Did you make it clear to the chief that the cub has not been offered as a gift?"

"I passed on your message," she replies, "and he is most grateful to receive both, as I said." This time she does not bother translating for her father.

McRory is about to protest further when an engine firing on only some of its cylinders breaks his concentration. He turns toward the source of the sound and watches as a black automobile and a military truck pull to a halt in the village square below. Through the bamboo bars of the balcony, Kumal also watches intently.

McRory walks to the open window and peers down as a native sergeant, wearing a dust-covered uniform, approaches the water buffalo convoy. The sergeant picks up the branches holding the contents of one of the carts and peers inside. The colossal head of the Buddha smiles up at the sergeant, who frowns and mutters something to the soldier standing beside him.

McRory has seen enough. "Excuse me, please," he says to Nai-Rea and bows slightly to the chief. He quickly steps down from the veranda and walks over to the sergeant.

"Can I help you, Captain?" he says.

The sergeant stands at attention and regards McRory with an icy glance.

"I am Sergeant Van Tranh. Second district."

"Oh, sorry, Sergeant. I'm afraid I'm not up on my military ranks. Didn't have the pleasure of serving in the Great War. What seems to be the trouble?"

Van Tranh looks McRory directly in the eyes and then stares pointedly at the smiling Buddha. He shakes his head and frowns.

"What do I see here? What is this object and what is it doing in this wagon, which I assume to be yours. I demand an explanation."

"Well, let me think." McRory looks thoughtful. He scratches his chin and pretends to be mulling the question over carefully. "Could it be a British subject in a safari outfit? Perhaps a creature from outer space?"

"I don't find you very amusing," the sergeant says. "In fact I find you extremely insolent."

"Awfully sorry, old chap."

"What I see here are sacred objects stolen from the temples."

"Is that what you see, Sergeant?" McRory says pleasantly. "How very interesting. Now what *I* see are some blocks of old stone that were rotting out there in the jungle."

"What is your name, sir?"

"Aidan McRory. British citizen." He winks. "Empire builder and all that."

Sergeant Van Tranh forages inside his tunic and produces a code book. After licking his thumb, he leafs through the pages, holding the book inches from his eyes and mouthing words aloud. He looks up finally with a satisfied smirk. "In accordance with section twelve, subsection 211 of the mineral resources act relating to the illicit use of a stone quarry, I request you show me your hands, Mr. McRory."

"Why on earth would I do that?"

"Just do as I say."

A group has formed around them, and villagers look on with incredulous shouts and whispers as handcuffs are placed on the white man's wrists. None of them have ever seen a white man treated with such boldness.

"Follow me," the sergeant says.

"Do I have a choice? You've handcuffed me."

"I hope you realize that you're in serious trouble, Mr. McRory."

"So it appears. Or at least so you say."

"You will regret your impudence. You people think you can come here and rape our country. Well, you are very much mistaken. You're going to pay dearly for this."

Kumal appears at the top of the veranda's steps and stares down at the pale upright man. He makes mewing sounds deep in his throat. His round greenish golden eyes watch the white man surrounded by soldiers and being led away, and the cub wants to go with him. But the steps are too steep. Kumal manages to make his way down the first two, backside first, with great difficulty. He is dragging the stool behind him, which is attached to a rope. The man must not leave him! The man must stay with him! As his feet touch the third step, the stool tips over and clatters down the stairs in front of him. It is no longer Kumal pulling the stool but the stool pulling Kumal. He lets out a shriek as he and the stool go tumbling down the steps and land in the dust near the base of the piles supporting the hut. Kumal, sprawled there and panting, watches as the man in brown opens the door of the black car and prepares to lead the white man inside.

A young cripple limps up to them on his crutches and hands McRory a necklace as an offering. He stammers a few words and bows deeply with his hands clasped together at his waist.

Nai-Rea, who has come up beside McRory, says, "A tiger ate his leg and he nearly died." She touches the cripple lightly on the shoulder and smiles warmly at him. "He gives you this charm to thank you and as a sign of his gratitude. He claims that it will bring you good fortune."

McRory puts the charm around his neck and smiles at Nai-Rea.

"How does it look on me?"

"It looks very good. It was meant for you."

"Well, it looks as if I'm going to need the luck."

Seeing Nai-Rea's face for the first time in the light, McRory is awed by the her luminous beauty, her large dark eyes, her elegant narrow nose, her full lips.

The pressure of Sergeant Van Tranh's hand on his arm brings him back to the present reality. He shakes off the man's hand and gets into the car unassisted. As the car pulls away in a cloud of dust, McRory looks at Nai-Rea. He then turns back and sees Kumal at the foot of the stairs, yanking on his rope and howling. The rope is still attached to the stool, which is now held firmly in place by the chief.

As the tiger cub lunges against the strength of the rope, wanting desperately to follow the car, he nearly strangles himself and rolls around in the dust. Hearing an unfamiliar voice directly above him, he looks up and sees the man in brown that put the white man in the car standing inches from him. His boots are brown and caked with dirt. Above Kumal's head, the sergeant produces a wad of colorful banknotes wrapped in brown paper. He hands the packet to the chief.

"The Administrator thanks you for your information," he says. "You have provided a great service to our land. We must catch these temple thieves and deal with them harshly."

The chief accepts the money, respectfully doffs his beret and stuffs the wad of money inside it. The medals make a chinking sound as he places the beret back on his head.

"We know our Lord by the gifts He brings," the chief says, smiling his teeth-blackened smile. "The Lord is good."

The sergeant returns to the car, and Kumal, at the chief's feet, almost under his sandals, continues to stare after the car until it disappears in the distance. He lets out a long, low moan.

* * *

As the shifting chords of evening begin to settle on the jungle and bring with them a symphony composed of the nocturnal animals, the silhouettes of the eighteen Buddhas lining the bridges are just beginning to fade in the gathering dusk. Moonlight reflects in the ruts left by the wagons in the soft clay of the trail. Leaping out of the ferns, two moving silhouettes, one large and the other small, appear on the path. Her back raised with tension, the Tigress approaches the tracks and sniffs them, and Sangha, watching her closely, also sniffs the tracks. The far off echo of Kumal's cries for help reach her. They are not any cub's cries: she knows the difference. She raises her head and gives an answering cry. Sangha, tail between his hind legs, moves close to his mother. He, too, has heard his brother's cries.

On the veranda Kumal is now wearing an iron chain. "*Aoooo! Aoooo! Aoooo!*" he cries, staring toward the forest. His mind carries images of the white man, of his mother, his brother, his father—all of them gone now. He is alone. The aloneness is another new thing in his very brief life, and he does not like this new thing at all. He continues to cry into the deepening twilight.

In the next room, the chief is unconcerned with Kumal's troubles as he counts his money. He is too absorbed to hear the cub's cries, but Kumal's cries are heard. At the Bridge of Eighteen Buddhas, his desperate entreaties reach his mother's ears. She answers at the top of her lungs, her head raised to the dark blue sky.

"*Ah-oom! Ah-oom!*"

The Tigress takes off at full speed, followed by a very determined but less than graceful Sangha, and she crosses the bridge in an orange-black blur of motion, bent on rescuing her son.

The villagers, too, have heard the Tigress, and panicked, they come rushing out of their huts armed with machetes, rakes and hoes. The chief, having counted his money and locked it in a drawer, has joined the crowd that rushes to the end of the village. Napoleon, his shoulder wrapped in a bloody rag, limps along in the rear and uses his rifle as a cane. His dog trails at his heels.

Sangha is not able to keep up with his mother and is forced to remain behind in the forest, hidden in the tall grass. Too frightened to make a sound, he lies on his belly, shivering. He watches his mother move swiftly, belly low, to the edge of the forest. She growls and ventures into the open ground of a freshly harvested rice paddy. Silhouetted against the sky, on a mission ignited in her by the sounds of her son's distress, she keeps moving toward the huts.

Kumal has sensed the presence of his mother and yanks on his chain, whimpering and writhing for release. He presses up against the back of the railing and tries to get a glimpse of her. With a final frantic pull against his restraint, he stumbles through the bars and falls. He is hanging from the chain in midair, suspended by his neck, moving in slow circles and squealing.

The Tigress stops dead in her tracks when she hears her son's cries of distress, but she is suddenly alert to other sounds in the distance—sounds of danger. She cranes her neck, rises on her hind legs and emits a low, sustained growl. She hears a metallic clamoring, which increases in intensity as she listens, and spots of light appear as moving circles that puncture the night.

On the outskirts of the village, beyond the range of the Tigress' vision, peasants have lit torches and they form a line of fire as they advance. The women chip in and create a deafening cacophony of sounds made up of gongs, pots and pans, cauldrons, and boisterous chants. The chief blows loud reports on his bugle, from which hangs the banner of the 2nd Chasseurs-Alpins. The Tigress can now see the glow of the flames. She continues to advance but stays low to the ground and moves with silent stealth. The sounds grow steadily louder, and the Tigress growls again, deep in her throat. Slowly she begins to back off.

Kumal, still spinning around on the end of his chain, cries out for his mother. He cries out for his brother. He recalls his father in battle, the popping sound, the flash of light, and his father falling to the ground. Kumal also cries out for him. He cries out for the pale upright man who was taken away from him.

For an instant his mother flashes across his line of vision and he can see a group of upright creatures hurling their torches toward her. He howls with all of the fury his small body contains. The dark man with the limp steps forward and aims and fires at his mother's retreating form. As quickly as she entered Kumal's line of vision she is gone, swallowed by the forest.

7

After coping with Kumal for two days, the chief decides that the cub must go. Always greedy for money, he realizes that he has just found a new source of income. When Zerbino, an animal tamer whose circus is in the village for an indefinite stay, shows interest in the cub, they quickly strike a bargain. The wrinkled hand of the chief accepts a thick roll of banknotes from the tamer. Zerbino wears a cape, a long black mustache with wing tips, and black boots, adorned with silver-plated tops. He refers to himself in the third person, as "The great Zerbino, world famous animal tamer, magician, knife thrower and director of the Great Zerbino Circus." Assuredly a mouthful of an introduction, but Zerbino manages it in one smooth-flowing breath. He watches with ill-concealed impatience as the chief licks his thick thumb and counts the money.

"You ask a lot for a cub," Zerbino says.

"You won't be disappointed," the chief assures him. "He is already an aggressive bundle of energy who will soon grow into a powerful male tiger. You have a bargain, my good friend."

The chief finishes counting the banknotes for the second time and glances at the animal tamer with his tooth-blackened smile. "We know our Lord by the gifts He brings. The Lord is good."

Zerbino turns away in disgust and walks out of the straw hut into the intense noonday sun. He approaches a wooden crate placed on the ground beside a small red truck. There are holes drilled in the top of the crate, and in bold red letters it is labeled: *Savon le Chat*. He unceremoniously dumps Kumal inside, and the cub scratches himself and moans.

Zerbino squats beside the crate and spits in the dust. "You better not let me down, little one," he says. "I paid dear for you and I have big plans for your future."

In the shadow of a thicket, not fifty yards away, the Tigress' golden eyes are fixed on this scene. Only her tail moves, twitching agitatedly. Sangha hops to the left and the right in an attempt to catch her tail in his teeth. The Tigress ignores him and continues to stare at the crate that holds her captive son. She pants and waits, in a position to spring.

When the crate is placed in the truck's flatbed and the truck, coughing and sputtering, begins to move forward, the Tigress makes her move. Sangha stumbles along behind, trying to keep pace with her. Kumal is tossed around like a sack of potatoes by the jolting of the truck as it rolls along the road full of potholes. Claws bared, he manages to get up on his hind legs against the walls of the crate, and through a hole he can see his mother running at full speed in pursuit of the truck. Behind her, rapidly losing ground, is his brother, Sangha. Kumal lets out a piercing howl.

Little by little, the Tigress is gaining on the truck. Kumal scratches on the crate and his howls become cries for help and deliverance. Two dozen long, gliding strides bring the Tigress alongside, and with one large leap she lands on the flatbed and rolls over twice before regaining her balance. She grabs the crate, which was not firmly tied down, in her enormous paws. She claws and bites at the rope and tries to widen the holes by tearing apart the boards.

Inside the crate Kumal is going wild. He meows, growls, scratches and bites the wood, attempting with every last ounce of his cub's strength to get to his mother. He wants to do everything he can to help her in her struggle to liberate him. In his brand-new world he has experienced freedom, and he has now felt the impact of its withdrawal. He desperately wants his freedom back.

Through the cracked rearview mirror, Zerbino gapes in astonishment when he catches a glimpse of the big cat on the flatbed, grappling with the crate. His silver-toed boot floors the gas pedal as he turns the wheel back and forth, causing the truck to fishtail. It continues erratically down the road and sends up a cloud of dust. Even so, the Tigress manages to cling to the flatbed as she sends up a blood-chilling roar.

Wearing a fixed and yet maniacal grin, Zerbino jams the steering wheel all the way to the left; the truck comes perilously close to flipping over, and the Tigress loses her balance, slips and falls halfway off the back. She manages to lurch forward with a powerful thrust and tries to maintain a grip with her front paws. But when the truck dives into a deep pothole, the Tigress can no longer hold on. Kumal watches as his mother falls off the back and rolls over and over in the dust. After a moment she gets up on shaky legs and watches the receding truck. She then turns away and limps off. The dust of the road churning in the air blinds Kumal for a moment. Then he has a blurred image of his brother catching up to her in the road, and he can hear his brother's long, plaintive moan. Kumal's cries join Sangha's—cries of abandonment mixed with grief.

* * *

That evening, the truck bearing the *Savon le Chat* crate moves through the village to the Zerbino circus site. A peasant riding a bicycle follows close behind the truck. Two dozen ducks are hanging upside down from either side of the *dong raik* across his shoulders. As he bikes he whistles a cheerful tune. Each time the truck brakes, the peasant, who has no brakes, nearly collides with the truck, causing the ducks to quack hysterically as they swing dangerously close to the crate containing Kumal.

Hearing the loud quacking, the cub lifts an eyelid. He has been dozing in a corner of the crate, dreaming about coconuts and playtime in the fields with his brother Sangha. His eyes open wider. Next to one of the holes in the crate, he sees something orange no more than two inches from his snout.

"Quack quack quack!"

Kumal pulls back from the bars of the crate, and the duck quickly moves away from the hole. This curious winged creature is surrounded by other winged creatures, all of them hanging upside down. Kumal studies them with fascination. He is having another new experience in his very brief, but thus far eventful, life. His knowledge is expanding at blinding speed.

Each time the truck pulls away, the peasant loses more ground and the end of the bamboo stick strung with the bunch of ducks slips back farther from the crate until finally they pass from Kumal's view. The sound—*quack quack*—remains with him, though, and he somehow knows that it doesn't signal danger.

Down the road from where Zerbino parks the truck, a number of infantrymen are guarding McRory's wagons containing the statues stolen from the temple. The soldiers are gathered outside a building with the word "prison" printed in bold red letters on a sign that hangs above the door. An official car with a flag flying from the hood pulls up to the curb with a squeal of brakes. A sweaty Frenchman, bulging out of his white suit, emerges slowly and with difficulty from the rear. The soldiers come to attention as the European turns to Sergeant Van Tranh.

"Where have you put the prisoner, Sergeant?"

"In the general holding cell, Monsieur l'Administrateur."

"Very good." The European gives the man a curt nod. He walks over to the wagons, mopping at his brow with an embossed handkerchief, and pulls up one of the tarpaulins. He glances at the statues without expression and says to the sergeant, without bothering to look his way, "Has he had anything to eat?"

"We gave him some porridge but he wouldn't touch it. He's a very high and mighty fellow, Monsieur l'Administrateur. English, you know. He has an answer for everything."

The European ignores the comment. "I assume you've taken his shoelaces and his belt away."

"He has no belt."

"His shoelaces?" the European repeats impatiently.

"We have done everything you requested," Van Tranh replies.

"Splendid, splendid," the European says absently, continuing to stare at the statues.

When the European enters the prison and walks up to McRory's cell, the hunter is sitting on a dusty mud floor among chicken thieves and murderers. A day's growth of beard darkens his cheeks. Through the bars he stares inquisitively at the portly European who has just charged up to his cell. As soon as he spots McRory, the Administrator raises his arms in surprise; he smiles and dips his head in respect; he feigns regret.

"I cannot believe it! I simply cannot believe my eyes! The famous Aidan McRory in prison! What a ludicrous mistake has been made. Please accept my sincere apologies. Why wasn't I told you were here?"

"Well, now you know," McRory says with a grin. "And I don't mind telling you I'm glad to see you, whoever you are."

"Please forgive me, I'm Eugene Normandin, the Administrator of this district."

"Good to meet you, Normandin. I've never been happier to see an unfamiliar face."

Normandin gives a firm nod and aims an icy stare at Sergeant Van Tranh, who with sullen reluctance unbolts the cell door.

"This is simply absurd," the Administrator goes on. "Aidan McRory, of all people, in this terrible, foul place. My son is familiar with all of your books, you know. *The Lion Hunt, The Ivory Trail.* Two of his favorites. He's mad about them. And my wife, she reads them to him. He's still very young, you know—seven, no, eight now, just turned eight—but because of you he's set on becoming a gentleman adventurer."

Normandin breaks off, glances at McRory's feet and turns to the sergeant with a frown.

"Don't tell me you took Mr. McRory's shoelaces, you imbecile!"

"But Monsieur l'Administrateur—"

"Not another word out of you."

61

Once McRory's shoes are tied, he follows a smiling Normandin out of the front door of the prison. The soldiers stand rigidly at attention and the Administrator addresses them, wagging a plump finger for emphasis.

"A word of warning. You must be more careful in the future." He turns to the sergeant, shaking his head angrily, and adds, "This little escapade, if repeated, could cost you your rank."

"Yes, Monsieur l'Administrateur," Van Tranh says in a sullen whisper.

Normandin points a finger at the statues on the wagons. "I would like to see two or three of these," he says, "to put an official stamp on things. I'll send them to some museum back home. That should calm all the ruffled feathers. The French will love them. Don't you think, McRory?"

"I should imagine they will," the hunter replies. He hesitates. "What about the rest of them?"

Normandin shrugs. "Keep them. We'll list them as holiday souvenirs."

McRory regards the Administrator with surprise. "You mean I'm free to leave?"

Normandin playfully wags a finger at the prison behind them. "Unless you'd rather go back inside, you're free to go. A man of your stature should not be detained on a technicality."

"And the, ah, souvenirs?"

"As I said, they are yours. I imagine you will make good use of them." The Administrator's smile is sly.

McRory grasps the man's hand and gives it a vigorous shake. "How can I ever thank you? My boat sails the day after tomorrow and I was sure I'd be stuck here till I cleared this business up."

"Without my intervention, it would have been much longer than that."

"Much longer," Sergeant Van Tranh cannot resist adding.

Normandin clears his throat, clearly ill at ease. He exchanges a quick, furious glance with Van Tranh, who immediately responds to the Administrator's unspoken appeal.

"I'm afraid, sir," he says, addressing the Administrator, "that we cannot permit Mr. McRory to leave the country just yet. Not until the paperwork is complete."

"What paperwork?" McRory asks.

"You know, the usual bureaucratic tangle," Normandin says with a shrug.

McRory nods. "I see."

"Do you really?" Normandin says anxiously. "I feel absolutely terrible about this. There is a mountain of red tape, even in this part of the world. You practically need some sort of official permission to blow your nose."

"No need to feel terrible," McRory tells him. "It's a relief just to be out of that hellhole. I'm grateful." He holds a hand up, palm outward as though swearing an oath. "And I promise never to steal another chicken."

"You're actually grateful?" Normandin says, missing McRory's stab at humor. "I'd think you would be most upset and simply too polite to show it."

"Believe me, I'm grateful, Normandin."

"Good. Then that gives me the courage to make a request."

"Just ask," McRory says. "You know I'll do whatever I can."

But Normandin being a European of a certain background, who believes that courtly manners are everything, has to steal up to the request in his own elaborate way. "It seems almost supernatural that a great hunter should be sent to me just at this moment in time. Kind fate has intervened in my behalf once again."

McRory regards him curiously. "I'm afraid I don't follow you."

"Well, you see, I'm in desperate need of a tiger. I would be forever in your debt if you could acquire one for me, and I am prepared to use whatever blandishments are necessary." He clears his throat. "I'm attempting to arrange a tiger hunt for His Excellency. Very frankly, it would be a great feather in my cap."

Standing near the prison entrance, Sergeant Van Tranh watches with murder in his eyes as the two men walk away, chatting like two gentlemen.

* * *

Kumal shakes feverishly as he hears the boards of his crate being pried off, and he tries to shrink into an invisible ball when the cover is removed. The upright creature with an emaciated face and a black mustache with wing tips stares down at him. Kumal returns his stare warily. The creature's hair is greasy and wavy and parted in the middle, and his terrible smile, more a snarl than a smile, sends shivers through the cub. He has just learned a valuable new lesson: not all upright creatures are kind like the pale man, and this creature has the smell and look of danger.

The man's ringed hand comes nearer, grabs Kumal roughly by the scruff of the neck and he shows off the pink-bellied, spitting kitten like a trophy.

"Saladin, I want to introduce you to our new man-eater," Zerbino says to the magician in his troupe.

Furtively, Kumal takes in a ragged little group of night creatures assembled under the filthy canvas of a tent—rodents, small monkeys, unfamiliar-looking birds with their wings tied to their breasts. Beyond them, he sees the cages of a traveling menagerie and can make out the silhouettes of animals whose eyes are glowing in the darkness. The human voices emerge from the gloom.

"Where did you find him?" the magician says, a smirk twisting his lips. "In the toy department?"

Zerbino spits on the ground. "He's fierce enough. Don't you worry."

Madame Zerbino, standing beside Saladin, studies the cub with interest. "He's cuddly and cute—at least he *looks* cuddly. Does he have a name?"

"Well, I've been thinking about it," Zerbino says as he gives the kitten a hard slap on the rump. "I decided the name for him is Kumal. Kumal fits him."

"Why Kumal?" Saladin asks.

"No particular reason except that it sounds right. Look at his round exotic eyes. The name is exotic like his eyes. It's the perfect name for a little man-eater."

The man with the black wing tips above his lips and the hideous smile now turns the baby tiger toward him.

"You are in the presence of the great Zerbino," he says, his voice deep and self-loving. "I am director of the Great Zerbino Circus and I'm a world famous animal tamer, magician and knife thrower."

He turns the squirming tiger cub toward an Annamese woman dressed in a short riding skirt, who is several months pregnant. "Meet Madame Zerbino," he says. "She is a skilled contortionist, equestrian, dancer, cashier and accountant. If you perform well for us, she will see that you're well fed."

He touches the round belly of his wife. "And cooking in her oven is the future son of Zerbino."

"Or daughter," she corrects him.

He flashes a sharp look at her.

"*My son*," he emphasizes. "Zerbinetto, future juggler and trapeze artist *extraordinaire*."

A burst of flame startles Kumal into a loud, prolonged growl. A Hindu with dark, disturbing eyes, dressed in a turban and faded, baggy Turkish trousers, emerges from the shadows. He exchanges a look with

Madame Zerbino and she smiles at him, her eyes alive with feeling.

Zerbino addresses Kumal. "This is not the Saladin you saw before who claimed I bought you at a toy store. No, this is the fire-eating, sword-swallowing Saladin, Madame Zerbino's cousin. This Saladin who stands before you is the vicious Ottoman Strangler."

As Kumal cringes deeper into Zerbino's firm grasp, Saladin swallows a gulp of gas and blows out a spray, which he ignites in a burst of flame. He approaches the terrified tiger cub and grasps him roughly by the back of the neck. Kumal knows suddenly that this creature is much worse than the one with the terrible smile; he recoils and hisses, twisting around in the man's arms and struggling with all his cub's strength. His teeth, pointy and sharp as needles, dig into Saladin's first finger, causing the man to scream in pain. Kumal experiences yet another new sensation—a surge of power that accompanies his aggression—but this is quickly dispelled by a kick from Saladin, which sends him sprawling against the iron bars. He is quickly locked inside.

The magician glares at him. He squats down and puts his face inches from the cage. "The sooner you learn it's not the tigers that run the show, the better for you. The next time you try something it won't go so easy for you...."

Silence returns to the menagerie as the two upright male creatures and the woman leave. Kumal gingerly rises to his feet. He wobbles two steps forward, but feeling an attack of dizziness he abruptly lies back down. He looks up at the bars of the cage next to his, and discovers an old tiger staring back at him. Kumal, continuing to stare, makes a soft mewing sound. A wave of hope washes over him. The old tiger reminds Kumal of his father. Again he struggles to his feet and comes forward, his meows increasing in volume.

"Me-owww. Me-owww," he cries out, keeping his eyes fastened on the old tiger.

Kumal watches with fascination as the ancient one slowly rises unsteadily to his feet. He walks listlessly to the other end of his cage and lies back down, turning his back on the little tiger. Kumal puts his paws on the bars of his cage and tries to shake them.

"Me-owwww….Me-owwww…" he pleads, but the old tiger does not move.

Kumal stands at the bars a moment longer, continuing to whimper, and then retreats to the corner of his cage. A huge sigh causes his little body to shudder. He curls up and stares into space, occasionally sighing, but no longer whimpering. Resignation is setting in. He knows that he is now truly alone, and this new knowledge is beyond the weight of sadness. He has no idea what it means. He grabs his paw and brings it to his mouth. He begins sucking it and after a while he slowly closes his eyes.

8

The following morning, Sangha and the Tigress are moving along a trail foraging for food. Between wind sprints, the cub slows down to inspect insects that cross his field of vision. He then runs full out and does circles around his mother. The vigilant Tigress keeps a close eye on her young as he playfully chases a butterfly.

Suddenly Sangha lets out a yelp and the Tigress lopes over to investigate. The cub is trying to extricate his paw from a net where the butterfly has landed. Pots and cattle bells are attached to the net and bang loudly against one another, creating a terrific din. The Tigress, her head tilted to one side, stops and looks uncomprehendingly at the net several yards in front of her, blocking the way to the forest. Just as her ears prick up to the distant sound of human voices responding to the clamor caused by Sangha as he wrestles with the net, the cub manages to pull free. Mother and child flee at full speed.

Later in the morning, safely removed from the threat of upright creatures, they once again amble peacefully along the trail—still hungry but not yet hungry enough to seek out a kill. Sangha trots along out in front. He stops and looks back at his mother, who has paused behind him. She is standing stock-still, her tail twitching furiously. She sniffs the air and listens intently. Sangha's eyes are fastened to her as he, too, sniffs the air. After a moment, the Tigress drops her head, seemingly satisfied that no danger lurks in the thick forest along the trail. She trots ahead again at a leisurely pace. Sangha again leads the way along the leafy trail. He has learned that he likes leading his mother. It makes him feel strong and in command.

He is about to veer off the trail in pursuit of a large purple butterfly when he hears a rustling of branches and a loud thud from behind that cause him to whip around and growl deep in his throat. He swings his head left and right, and lets out a series of surprise bleats. His mother has disappeared. Slowly, belly low to the ground, Sangha retraces his steps, sniffing the ground as he goes. At the far left edge of the trail, he peers into a deep rectangular pit; the Tigress is trapped inside, prowling back and forth, leaping against the steep walls with her claws in an attempt to find a way out of the trap.

The tiger cub mews frantically as he watches his mother's futile thrashings about and hears her guttural growls. In his panic, he leans too far forward over the edge, slips and with a yowl falls into the hole. Immediately he runs to the Tigress and buries himself in the warmth of her belly. Seconds later a shadow falls over mother and child, and they look up to see a human form standing over the pit.

Aidan McRory briefly contemplates the cub and its mother, the cub wide-eyed and the big mother cat snarling and staring up at him with her golden eyes. He lifts his arm in the motion of throwing a ball, and the Tigress and her cub can hear the creaking sound of a pulley. They watch as a bamboo grate is lowered above them, forming a lid to the trap. The Tigress rears up on her hind legs and lets out a deafening roar.

A female upright creature with long dark hair joins the pale man at the edge of the trap. She smiles at the hunter.

"The villagers are happy to see you again."

"I'm more happy for them than for me," he says. "I guess you could say my stay has been extended by—I think it's called—'circumstances beyond my control.'"

As Nai-Rea and McRory stare into the pit, they are joined by villagers who seem to have appeared out of nowhere. They point and jeer at the trapped tigers and clap their hands like children at play. A young boy pitches a rock into the pit and McRory gently pushes the boy away.

"None of that," he remonstrates. "Never disturb the animals."

He looks at Nai-Rea, who translates for him, and the boy runs off laughing.

She turns to McRory. "My father wants to thank you for your assistance. He will show you the temples upriver where there are many statues."

McRory regards her. "The chief deceived me. Because of him I ended up in jail."

"My father was simply doing business the village way."

"I see."

"I know it's difficult for you to understand. You take a payment from one side and then from the other."

"Civilization is not built on practices like that."

She studies his features with a sad smile. "You're angry aren't you, Mr. McRory?"

"Not really. New customs are a learning process. I may not approve of them but one must acclimate oneself. I guess you could call me a student of human nature. It's a sobering discipline."

"Are you willing to accept the chief's offer to go upriver?"

"Aren't the temples very far away?"

"Oh no. Only about three weeks by canoe."

McRory smiles. "I have a feeling you and I have very different concepts of distance and time. Three weeks in the jungle sounds like a lifetime to me."

"You went on long safaris in Africa."

"That's true. But I knew the terrain."

"You will not be disappointed, Mr. McRory. I promise you."

He studies her, feature by feature, finding her increasingly fascinating—beautiful, complex, and, he senses, perhaps as morally neutral in her own way as the chief.

"Where did you learn your English?" he asks.

"His Excellency petitioned the Australian priests to open a school here. He does not like the French and despises their language."

"I can appreciate his position. His country hasn't had an easy time with the French. What else did the priest teach you?"

"To beware of white men," she answers with a charming smile.

McRory nods gravely. "Very sound advice."

* * *

That evening, in the home of Monsieur l'Administrateur Eugene Normandin, a white-haired lap dog of obscure origins named Bitzy is busy yapping in the arms of a small boy wearing a sailor suit. The eight-year-old Raoul Normandin and his dog are peeking through a door left ajar into another room, where Aidan McRory paces back and forth. Raoul knows that the man is the famous author of the books his mother reads to him over and over again, and that he is one of the world's great adventurer-hunters. He can hardly contain his excitement. Raoul wants to go inside and introduce himself, but he fears his father's wrath. He will have to wait until the moment his parents deem proper. It has been drilled into the boy that doing the proper thing at all times is a crucial social commandment, but the truth is, it has never quite taken with Raoul, who is certain that true adventurers are never so very proper.

The great hunter, McRory, examines the pompous décor of the spacious office while he waits for the Administrator. A map of Indochina is hanging on the wall, along with several posters advertising cruises to Southeast Asia—A TASTE FOR HIDDEN ADVENTURE? DISCOVER THE SPLENDORS OF THE HIDDEN TEMPLES. McRory is bent over a large-scale model of a road that cuts through the jungle to the temples when the door opens and Normandin comes rushing toward him, his arms outstretched.

"Well, my friend, give me the news." He wags his finger in mock gravity. "And please reassure me that the news is good."

"We have a tiger, Monsieur l'Administrateur. It was caught in our trap yesterday morning."

"Excellent, excellent." But the fat man frowns and fidgets with a button on his jacket. He is worried; so much of his future is riding on his plan working to perfection; there must not be any slipups.

"Do you think one tiger is enough?" he asks.

"That depends on your guest. How good a shot is he?"

"There's no way I can know for certain, but I'm not sanguine. His Excellency's father was an extremely skilled hunter." Normandin sighs and his shoulders slump forward. "Indeed, the father had many outstanding qualities, but I'm afraid none of them appear to be hereditary."

Normandin shifts his gaze to the model McRory was studying when he entered the room.

"I saw you looking at it when I came in," he says. "What do you think?"

"I was admiring the careful workmanship, the attention to detail."

"Yes, impressive, isn't it?" Normandin's huge frame seems to balloon out even more with pride. "It will be an enormous undertaking, but if His Excellency agrees to building the road, think of the benefits. Soon there will be no need to break up the temples and ship them to London. London will gladly come here to see them. The future of tourism, McRory, depends on the construction of this road. A vast wave of people with money will troop here willing to crane their privileged necks at anything that smells of culture. This road"—he taps the model lovingly—"is going to make it happen."

A pretty woman in a sheer summer dress stands smiling in the doorway. "Poor Mr. McRory," she says in a wry tone, with hints of laughter just beneath the surface. "Eugene, if you had to bore the poor man to distraction with the splendors of La Route Normandin, you might at least have waited till he'd had some lunch. Lectures go down better on a full stomach."

"Have I been boring you, McRory?"

"Not at all."

Normandin turns to his wife with an ironic bow and the sweep of his right hand. "My dear Mathilde...my dear, may I introduce Aidan McRory? He has kindly offered to organize the hunt for His Excellency."

"I know who he is, Eugene."

McRory takes her hand and kisses it, looking steadily into her greenish-hazel eyes. He says, "I take it you don't support our little enterprise."

"The road through the jungle? It's hardly little. And indeed I do support it. I support anything that will get me out of this Godforsaken country and back to civilization. So mind you, make a success of the hunt. If His Excellency agrees to let the new road cross his land, it could be our ticket back to Paris."

"I would hate to disappoint you, Madame Normandin. I promise to do my level best."

* * *

At dawn the next day, the brightening sky filters through the bamboo roof and the interior of the pit is streaked with the first ribbons of sunlight. The Tigress paces back and forth, back and forth. She growls, snorts and roars. Sangha watches her as she attempts to scale the vertical wall. She tries to use a stone that juts out from the wall as a stepping stone, but the pressure of her great weight dislodges the stone and she tumbles to the ground. She paces again, growling, then attempts to scale another wall of the pit. She rises on her hind legs and grasps a tangle of roots. Lifting herself slowly and panting heavily, she manages to reach the bamboo grid. Sangha leaps up and grasps his mother's tail between his teeth and hangs on for dear life. He feels himself being lifted toward the opening, but his weight added to his mother's proves to be too great. The tangle of roots breaks away from the wall, and the Tigress and her cub fall to the bottom of the pit.

* * *

Four hours later, the midday sun beats down on the plain, and a cloud of dust billows on the horizon as, shining brightly in the distance, a white Rolls Royce carrying His Excellency and his female companion moves slowly along the pothole-filled road. A few miles ahead of them servants finish setting a table under the shadow of a large Banyan tree. The abundance of champagne, the Sevres crystal glasses and the fine silver suggest that this is no ordinary occasion. This is the great royal hunt of the season.

When Normandin sees the limousine approaching, a banner with a coat of arms tied to the hood ornament and fluttering in the breeze, he rushes up to the banquet table waving his arms excitedly.

"Champagne," he shouts in French. "Get out the champagne, for God's sake. *Sortez le Champagne! Sortez le Champagne!*"

Normandin is wearing his dress uniform, and large perspiration stains darken the armpits. A short time in the sun has left him looking wilted. The old chief has polished to a high sheen the medals that decorate his ceremonial beret.

"And the chorus," Normandin continues to shout. *"Where is the chorus?"* He claps a hand to his head like the victim of foul play in a silent movie. *"Ou est la chorale?"*

On a platform in the shade, old men in tri-colored sarongs tune their instruments. The village children hold small flags in their hands. The chief, wearing a vacant smile, comes to attention, causing the polished medals on his ceremonial beret to jingle. Under her wicker parasol, Madame Normandin's slightly pink face leans toward McRory, but his attention is divided and mostly elsewhere. He is intrigued by the graceful profile of the choir director—the chief's daughter, Nai-Rea.

"What is it about these hideous statues that attracts you?" Madame Normandin asks.

McRory answers absentmindedly, his gaze fixed on the platform. "My motives aren't very mysterious," he answers, "and I'm afraid they're not aesthetic—perhaps not even honorable. Statues are less work than hunting for ivory, and they sell for a great deal more money. Besides, ivory seems to be out of fashion these days. Increasingly, people object to the slaughter of elephants. I guess that about sums it up."

"You can hardly blame people for objecting to killing elephants."

"I don't. Statues have captured my attention."

Madame Normandin tucks a heavy ivory bangle into her sleeve and regards him closely. She says, "After all your adventures it must feel very tame poking about vine-smothered temples."

McRory pulls his eyes away from the platform and turns to her. "It does feel very different, Madame Normandin, but I like that. After all my years in Africa, I think I'm ready for something new—new and tame."

The limousine negotiates the final potholes and draws up near the Banyan tree. Normandin mops his brow and waves furiously for his wife to join him.

Madame Normandin rises and says after a pause, "Well, I beg you, forget statues today and just be the great hunter. Put a smile on His Excellency's face and I could be back in furs on the Rue de Lapaix by Christmas. You cannot imagine how I dream of being cold again and how delicious it will feel."

McRory stands and watches her walk off, fanning herself vigorously. When she has joined her husband, he strolls over to the platform, hands deep in his pockets.

"Well, well," he says, "fancy seeing you here. You seem to be a woman of many talents."

Nai-Rea smiles at him. "Not really. What is it they say? Many trades but master of none."

"I think it's 'jack of all trades and master of none.'"

She blushes. "I'll remember that next time."

"You impress me as having many talents, Nai-Rea."

Her smile grows wider. "Are you flirting with me, Mr. McRory?"

He hesitates as though in deep thought. "Why I certainly hope so."

"Seriously, Mr. McRory, I hope all your activities in our country will be rewarded. You are a good person. I can tell. You have a good heart."

He regards the young woman and her spectacular beauty.

"Would it be too much trouble to call me Aidan?" he says. "Mr. McRory sounds like an old Irish soak on his last legs. Do you think you could at least try?"

"I'll consider it," she says.

"You know, I've thought about your father's offer to see the temples upriver. I must say it's tempting. I've been told the statues are more beautiful than any I've seen yet."

As he waits for her reaction, Normandin shouts hoarsely, "Music! Music!"

"Tell me, Nai-Rea, it appears I'll be staying on for a while. Do you think I could persuade you to act as my guide? You see, I really need someone who speaks English and can translate for me." He raises a hand and adds with a grin, "This, by the way, is not an attempt at flirtation. It's a sincere offer."

Her manner suddenly grows awkward, as though she is struggling to sort out her feelings, but her expression reveals nothing.

"You will have to ask my father."

"The chief owes me a favor."

"That is between you and him."

"Let's say I ask and he agrees to let you be my guide. Would you be willing to sign on?"

But the moment is lost: the musicians, somewhat on key, begin playing the opening notes of the *Marseillaise*. Nai-Rea hastily cues the chorus after a few beats and the village children strike up the local version of the French national anthem.

"Allons z'enfants de non-Kyn Tuy...y...y...y...Le jour de gloire est arrivé."

Normandin hurries over to the white Rolls Royce with gold fenders, which has just parked in the shade of the Banyan tree. A majordomo in the dress uniform of an English gamekeeper stands on the running board, a pair of Purdy rifles slung across his shoulder. His expression when he gazes at Normandin is perfectly blank.

His Excellency, a young Asian, short and slightly plump, climbs down from the car. He is dressed in the European style, perhaps a little too immaculately. His features are still almost childish; his cheeks are smooth and nearly hairless; and his full lips are held in a perpetual pout as though the world is a disappointment to him. He has recently celebrated his thirty-third birthday.

The village children ogle the youthful potentate and raise their voices a few decibels:

"Pres de nous dans la color ie——ie——s'en vient notre excellence bien-aimée..."

Following His Excellency out of the car is a slender young woman in high-heeled boots. She is dressed elegantly, her features are refined, if a trifle sharp, but they somehow miss beauty or even prettiness.

Madame Normandin leans toward McRory, who has moved up close to the Rolls Royce.

"Do you see?" she says in a whisper. "English shoes, English clothes, English automobile. Even his major-domo is dressed in Saville Row. It's all done quite deliberately to offend us. Also, I suspect, to offend the memory of his father, who was a Francophile."

"The girl looks French enough," McRory observes.

"He ran across her in Paris, dancing at the Moulin Rouge. Eugene heard about their little fling and arranged to have her brought here for a visit. He thinks she might win His Excellency over to our point of view, but looking at her, I doubt it."

As they watch His Excellency and the former cabaret dancer, she twists her ankle and starts to stumble.

"*Zut!*" she shouts. "*Attendez!* Wait!"

His Excellency pauses with weary, exquisite courtesy.

"What is it now, my dear?"

"I've broken my heel!"

He sighs softly and moves on.

McRory shoots a look at Madame Normandin and grins. "I'm not sure your husband's plan is working out," he says.

9

A shot rings out, and through the slits in the bamboo roof Sangha and the Tigress watch a green flare as it rises into the sky. They hear a pulley squeaking, and over their heads one side of the bamboo roof slowly lowers to the ground. The Tigress rises quickly to her feet, suddenly alert. A ramp has been put in place that leads out of the trap. Sangha observes his mother as she inches forward, sniffing suspiciously, on her guard. After a brief hesitation she walks carefully up the ramp and out of the hole. Sangha follows close behind her.

The great hunt, created for His Excellency, is about to begin. A horn blows in the trees, and from the top of a lookout post over the trap a spotter gives the signal. Sangha sees his mother take off into the thicket. The little tiger is hot on her heels.

The Normandin family is set to observe the hunt in a wicker rig, rocking to the gentle gait of an elephant draped in the colors of the French flag. The lap dog Bitzy is swaying in the arms of Raoul, the little boy with the sailor collar, who himself is swaying in the arms of Madame Normandin. Bitzy has his front legs up on a wicker armrest, yapping away steadily. Behind Madame Normandin, swaying and sweating copiously, her husband holds a parasol over her, shielding her from the sun.

Two more pachyderms lead the procession, harnessed for the hunt. McRory is in one, his Winchester at the ready. Alongside him, the other elephant sparkles in the sun, bejeweled with precious stones and gold, and there are banners with a coat-of-arms affixed to its head. Under the canopy, regal in a Louis XV armchair, His Excellency is holding a rifle with a mother-of-pearl stock. His companion, the former cabaret dancer, sways behind him, looking slightly pale.

"Are you all right?" he asks her, hearing her soft moan.

"It's just the swaying. It reminds me of being at sea."

"You don't have to do this, you know. Why not go back to the car?"

"Oh, I wouldn't miss it for the world!"

She gives him a game smile, but as he turns away she rolls her eyes and frowns.

The line of beaters moves through the bamboo forest with the practiced ease born of long experience. The natives have zinc basins, drums, muskets, cattle bells, corrugated sheet metal plates, ancient automobile horns and novelty shop rattles. The noise makers' and criers' task will be to herd the tiger back toward the clearing so that a clean shot can be fired.

The Tigress creeps out into an area clear of trees but strewn with fallen rocks. She freezes; her ears quiver; she listens intently, and growls low in her throat. From her left she can hear the clamor of the beaters fast approaching her, and on the other side she sees the elephants advancing toward her. She senses that she is cornered. Just then, Sangha catches up to her, running erratically, so tired that he can hardly stand. She seizes him by the scruff of the neck and leaps up onto a narrow ledge on the hillside where she deposits him in a cave under two big boulders. The cub's legs are trembling and he whimpers piteously.

No sooner is he settled than the heavy tread of the approaching elephants vibrates along the ledge. Sangha watches his mother as she moves away, back down the incline, her tail whipping behind her. He is too tired to follow her, and besides, he knows that she wants him to remain hidden. He continues to watch her as she moves out of his line of vision.

The Tigress lets out a muffle growl. As she crouches close to the ground, she knows that the upright enemy is everywhere and there will be no easy escape. There are upright creatures to the left and right of her. There is no safe retreat; the hills are steep, impossible to climb without being in the open, and if she tried she would be an easy target. She has no choice but to brave the danger and charge directly into the midst of the enemy, hoping that somehow her speed and the surprise of her advance will take her beyond them to the dense covering at their rear. Thoughts of escape glow brightly in her golden eyes, mixed with thoughts of savage revenge on the upright creatures.

Moving slowly forward, she watches the elephants fan out in a semicircle before her. The elephant covered with gold and jewels advances straight toward her, its trunk held high.

Normandin, his eyes fixed on McRory, gestures with a nod. McRory returns his nod and shoulders his rifle, ready to play the backup role—to be prepared for any inadequacy on the part of Normandin's guest, His Excellency. The youthful leader is quick to interpret the silent exchange between the two men and a shadow crosses his face.

"McRory," Normandin finally shouts, having witnessed His Excellency's reaction. "No!" He signals the hunter to lower his rifle.

At that instant the Tigress springs forward, reaching full speed within two strides. She sees the man's rifle pointed at her; she sees the flash of light as she moves in a zigzag pattern—a black-and-orange blur of motion. The shot rings out in Sangha's hiding place and he jumps as if the bullet had struck him. He whines and hunkers down deep in his hole.

His Excellency's servants roll a moveable stairway to the side of his glittering elephant and he starts slowly down the stairs as everyone claps and congratulates him on his shot. At the bottom step McRory hands him a revolver.

"For the coup de grâce, Your Excellency," he says, his expression bland, with perhaps the merest hint of amusement in his eyes.

Normandin watches His Excellency stiffen, and fearing a repeat of the earlier near insult, he intercedes before the youthful leader can respond.

"Put the gun away, McRory," he says. "No need for it." He turns to the youthful potentate with an ingratiating smile. "As Your Excellency's father always said, 'One shot, one kill....' No true sportsman needs more than a single bullet."

His Excellency regards Normandin with mild annoyance. "I am not my father," he says.

"Of course not—who could be? Great man, great indeed. But you shoot like him...I can see that. With you it's bang...straight as an arrow."

A small smile appears on His Excellency's lips, but his eyes are cold and unresponsive. He says, "I would put it somewhat differently. I would say as straight as your proposed road through the sacred jungle of my ancestors."

Normandin starts to respond, then thinks better of it and remains silent.

"We are ready for you, Your Excellency," says a photographer in the youthful leader's retinue, who has finished putting a camera on a tripod. His Excellency nods, sadness suffusing his soft features. As is customary for such pictures, he poses by placing a foot on the body of the Tigress. He notices that there is a small pool of blood near the animal's ear and he quickly looks away.

Normandin is still fussing, desperate to make certain that this hunt is a little work of art with a happy end-ing, and will prove to be his and wife's passport back to Paris.

"But where is Your Excellency's guest?" he frets. "She really ought to be in the photograph."

His Excellency looks around for the former dancer. He sees her leaning over the edge of the wicker seat, looking as if she is about to be sick. He raises his brows slightly, a flicker of distaste darkening his features.

"Let her be," he says. "She has enough to contend with. Besides, she is not in any state to promote your cause. Not for a while anyway."

As Normandin starts to respond, the flashbulb pops, and everything seems to happen at once. From under His Excellency's foot the Tigress rears up with a mighty roar. His Excellency slips and falls into a mud puddle. The photographer emerges from beneath his black camera cloth cursing in French. The Tigress bleeding from her ear takes off into the thicket; and the native guards scream and fire at will. McRory shakes his head in disgust.

Normandin helps His Excellency to his feet and attempts to brush him off, but the young leader irritably shrugs off his ministrations.

"No harm done, Your Excellency," Normandin says, attempting a smile, which quickly falters.

"No harm is done to you, Monsieur l'Administrateur. But what will the people say about my sporting prowess? I fully expect to be a rich source of jokes for years to come. And justifiably so."

He touches his muddy garment with an ironic smile. For him, the only good result of his calamity is the opportunity to enjoy the fat man's obvious discomfort.

"But Your Excellency, the tiger is dead!"

"For a dead tiger it runs extremely fast."

Normandin turns to McRory for help, but the hunter simply shrugs and says nothing.

After the camera equipment and the regal stairway are reloaded on the bejeweled elephant, His Excellency climbs into his Rolls Royce with the ashen-faced former dancer. Normandin rushes forward, rubbing his hands together, and says, "The beast can't have got far. She is surely dead by now and close by. We will send you the skin."

His Excellency nods. "Yes, I rather suspect you will."

Normandin respectfully closes the door and the limousine rolls away through the tall grass. He turns to McRory, his face mottled with pink and red spots. "If we'd taken him fishing he would have fallen overboard. What a poor excuse for royalty he is."

In the distance there is the shrill sound of barking. Madame Normandin looks all around in panic and calls out, "That sounds like Bitzy. *Bitzy?* Where is my little puppy dog." She looks hard at her husband. "Eugene— Raoul was with you a minute ago. For God's sake, he's gone too! *Where is Raoul?*"

* * *

The sound of barking echoes through the little cave. Huddled in the cave's extreme rear, Sangha stares in terror at the opening. He sees a small dog, wagging its stumpy tail and barking furiously. Behind the dog, looking at him in wide-eyed curiosity, is a very small upright creature. Sangha tries to press himself into the rock and disappear as the small boy in a sailor suit begins to crawl toward him on all fours.

"Don't be afraid," the boy says. "I won't hurt you."

10

In the menagerie of the Zerbino circus, the old tiger looks with dead eyes at the neighboring cage. He observes the animal tamer pushing a bowl of food toward the tiger cub. While his wife watches, Zerbino examines the cub and shakes his head. Kumal lies on his side, his eyes half closed; his coat is dry and scruffy and he has grown thin in a matter of days.

"You must eat, Kumal," Zerbino says. "Otherwise, what good are you to me?"

"It's no use telling him such things," Madame Zerbino says. "He doesn't understand you. *Make him eat.* We spent good money on him."

The Turkish Strangler, otherwise known as Saladin, a pitchfork in hand, comes out of the shadows of the menagerie. Madame Zerbino casts an admiring glance his way as he approaches the cage, a look to which Zerbino is oblivious.

"Before long we'll have to find the old Chinaman who stuffed the jackal for us. He can fix up this old beast—a beautiful big hide. It should fetch a good price. It's perfect for a mantelpiece or a library."

The old tiger's morose, rheumy eyes follow them as they walk away. He sighs—a rumbling sound deep in his chest—and pushes his hindquarters against the bars of Kumal's cage. The cub's eyes have closed again and only a twitch of his ears reassures the old tiger that Kumal is still alive. Into Kumal's murky dreams of tumbling in tall grass with his brother creeps a steady beating noise—*splat, splat, splat, splat.* Reluctantly he gives up his dream and lifts one eyelid to contemplate the tail of the old tiger curling into his own cage. It is thumping the cage floor with a rhythmic insistence. Fascinated, Kumal opens his other eye. He doesn't move; only his eyes move. They follow the tail's metronomic movements, back and forth, back and forth.

On the other side of the bars, the old tiger watches out of the corner of his eye as Kumal sits up a little, now turning his head in time with the tail's dance, his round eyes suddenly filled with energy. In a swift swipe, he grabs at the tail with his paw, his childlike playful instincts winning out over his apathy. But the crafty old tiger keeps the tail out of his reach. Kumal stands, and his eyes glow with concentration. He leaps left and right, purring with pleasure like a child trying to grab the brass ring on a merry-go-round. He leaps and withdraws in an effort to fool the old tiger, then leaps again for the tail, which continues to elude him.

As Kumal goes on playing, feeling like a cub once more with no worry in the world beyond trying to catch the old tiger's tail, Zerbino announces into a megaphone: "Now, ladies and gentlemen, the moment you've been waiting for."

From a large rent in the traveling circus tent, the moon shines down from the Southeast Asian sky, highlighting Zerbino, who is wearing his best animal tamer's outfit complete with gold buttons and epaulets. With a theatrical flourish of his hands, he checks the solidity of the circular cage around the ring.

"This evening," he announces in a voice as deep and compelling as a country preacher's, "the great Zerbino is proud to present its audience with a savage killer...."

A dozen native villagers are sitting on wobbly benches looking glum as they listen to this speech.

"The most infamous of man-eaters," Zerbino continues, "this great beast strikes terror in the hearts of men. Prepare yourself, get ready for the thrill of a lifetime, for I give you...Bloody Caesar!"

As Zerbino is winding up his pitch, Saladin opens the cage over which a sign painted in gold and red reads: CAESAR, THE MAN-EATER. Saladin stares at the old tiger with open disgust and the animal stares back with dull, flat eyes. Saladin prods the recumbent tiger with his pitchfork. "Come on, on your feet, you lazy bum. Move it. Where do you think you are, a nursing home?"

He watches impatiently as the aged, arthritic animal struggles slowly to his feet. Ignoring the chickens hopping and pecking around him, the old tiger walks ponderously toward the scarlet curtain that separates the circus ring from backstage.

"Not that way," Saladin shouts. "Christ!"

The animal continues toward the curtain and is about to push it aside. Cursing, Saladin gives him a powerful shove toward the tunnel of iron hoops used for "wild" animals.

"The tunnel, the tunnel, you stupid beast," Saladin hisses. "What's wrong with you? You're a ferocious tiger, a killer of men—act like one!"

The old tiger glances toward Kumal's cage as he limps by. He sees that the cub is busily gobbling up all the food in his dish. The old tiger's mouth opens and his dull eyes brighten in a kind of smile.

* * *

At the same time the old tiger is set to perform on stage, Raoul Normandin is beside himself with joy. He has been given the gift of a lifetime—his very own baby tiger cub. In their few days together, he has already taught the tiger many games, including his favorite, Hide and Seek. Right now, his eyes closed and covered by his hands, he is standing in the closet of his bedroom, which is crammed with toys of every description and counting backwards.

"Thirteen, twelve, eleven, ten," he calls out. He can hear a slight rustling and continues to count. "Three, two, one. Coming, ready or not!"

He opens the closet door, steps out and surveys his bedroom with a squinty, concentrated look. He inches forward toward a miniature garage, flings open the door and peers inside. Empty. The boy's search is methodical but conducted in double time. He gets down on his hands and knees and crawls over to his bed. Lifting the cover, he peers underneath and pulls a painted wooden clown out of the dark and dusty recesses.

"I'm not looking for *you*," he says with evident disappointment to last year's favorite toy.

He rises and stares around his busy bedroom.

"Sangha. *Sangha.* Where are you?"

Raoul's eyes come to rest on a shelf crowded with stuffed animals—a family of monkeys, a black bear, a white rabbit, a Saint Bernard, a seal, a lion and an elephant. And...and...*what is that?*

Raoul's eyes light up.

"Sangha—I see you!"

A striped tail is peeking out from behind the elephant, a tiger cub's tail, and it hangs over the lip of the shelf, wagging back and forth. Laughing, the small boy rushes to the tiger cub and buries his face in his fur.

When playtime comes to a close and dinner is over and Raoul's face is washed and his teeth brushed, and the stately Normandin residence, a masterpiece of colonial architecture, is all in darkness, it is story time. Raoul lies propped up on pillows in anticipation, and Sangha, the great new love of his life, lies beside him. A sheet is pulled up to their necks. Sangha sucks on an empty baby bottle he holds in his paws. Sitting in the glow of a single lamp, Madame Normandin reads to her son from *The Lion Hunt*, by Aidan McRory. This is their third trip through the book, and Raoul never tires of it. If truth be told, neither does his mother.

"With two of our bearers dead and another savagely mauled," she reads softly, with an actor's emotion, "my tracker and I knew there was no time to lose. We had to rid the village of this bloodthirsty monster and our chance came sooner than we expected."

Bitzy is furiously scratching on the other side of the closed bedroom door and lets out little barks, but the household has learned the hard way (thanks to scratches, bites and broken objects) that the tiger cub and the dog are best kept separated. So Bitzy stations himself at the door as he does every night waiting for his mistress to emerge. He knows that the reward for his patience will be to spend the night snuggled in her bed.

"We had struck camp at dawn," she continues reading, "and only just set off when suddenly there was a movement in the rocks, and all at once the air was filled with roaring teeth and claws...." Madame Normandin glances up from the book, a line of irritation running between her eyes. "Oh do be quiet, Bitzy!"

"Don't pay any attention to him, Mother," Raoul says. "You're at the best part now." He absently strokes the cub's head as he listens.

Madame Normandin returns to the book. "With no time to aim, I brought the gun to my shoulder and fired. The bullet struck the man-eater full in the chest, and, with a dull thud, it fell at the feet of my tracker."

Raoul stares up at his mother, a frown shadowing his youthful features.

"Mother, I'm wondering about something."

"What is it, dear?" She inserts a finger in the page they're reading as a place marker.

"I never thought of those lions that get killed in the book—I never thought of them as cubs, like Sangha. I wouldn't want to see Sangha killed, not ever." He rubs Sangha's head vigorously and is rewarded with an answering purr.

"No one is going to kill Sangha," his mother says. "He is simply adorable."

"But how do you know? What about when he grows up? You said I won't be able to keep him then. What will happen to him?"

"That's something we can discuss with your father," his mother says, her usual response to difficult questions. "Do you want me to continue reading?"

"Yes," he answers, but with somewhat less than his usual enthusiasm.

"The beast rolled over," she reads, "and stared at me with its green pellucid eyes, extending and retracting his claws in the final throes of death. We stood there, silent, before the magnificent creature. Then, according to custom, I cut open the chest and gave the warm steaming heart to my client...."

Both Raoul and Sangha are nearly asleep, their eyelids growing heavy. Madame Normandin closes the book, turns the book to the back jacket and studies the photograph of Aidan McRory in his hunter's garb in fond contemplation. She turns out the light and removes the baby bottle from Sangha's paws. She plants a light kiss on her son's forehead and another on Sangha's snout.

"Good night, Raoul," she says. "Good night, Sangha. Pleasant dreams, my darlings."

* * *

For many days, Raoul has anticipated the coming Saturday evening. The great hunter and writer, Aidan McRory, has accepted an invitation to his house for dinner. It is hard for him to believe that the same man who wrote those wonderful books would be spending the evening in his home, eating dinner with his parents!

Raoul worked out a strategy that would allow him to take full advantage of the hunter's presence. Shortly before McRory's arrival, Raoul and Sangha created a space for themselves under the table in the dining room. They wait until the cocktail hour is nearly ended and then hide from view under the overhanging table-cloth. No more then fifteen minutes later they are surrounded by three pairs of adult feet, and his father's right foot is missing a shoe, which is pushed to one side. Around them house boys in white gloves are performing their silent ballet of service, and floating down to them is the voice of Raoul's father. "So how are you enjoying your extended stay?"

"Very much, as it happens. It's such a complete change from Africa. A good change in many ways."

"I hear that you've been keeping yourself entertained. Does that mean we're entitled to hope that you'll stay on for a while in our beautiful colony? It sounds as if you have plenty to keep you occupied."

"There is talk of a certain local beauty," Madame Normandin chimes in. She is sitting opposite the two men—"So that we can both gaze at your beauty, my dear," says Normandin, explaining the curious seating arrangement.

"There is always talk," McRory replies. "One should never put much stock in it."

"Someone said you were asking about the river region," Normandin says, quick to change the subject. "You know how gossip travels in small communities."

"I'm aware of it. In large communities, too, in my experience."

"Are you interested in the river region?"

McRory nods. "Yes. It has intriguing possibilities."

"I find that very interesting. Of course there are some exquisite temples upriver."

"So I have heard."

"But I must warn you, McRory, Sergeant Van Tranh is getting very hot under the collar. I'm not confident that he can be contained for long. I'm nominally his superior, but there's a military jurisdiction he can appeal to that lies beyond my control."

"I didn't know the Sergeant had any power."

"He has the power of the police behind him. I can be of only so much assistance to you."

While speaking, Normandin is searching with his stocking-covered feet for the shoe he removed.

"I wonder," he continues, "if there isn't a better way. It might make things much easier for you if you had some sort of official hat to wear. We could make you special advisor for hunting and the protection of flora. How does that sound?"

"It sounds rather long. What would it involve?"

Madame Normandin feels a foot rubbing slightly against hers. She suddenly flushes pink and sneaks a look at McRory, who continues to regard Normandin with polite interest. What a cool customer, she thinks, with a thrill of admiration and excitement.

Normandin, still groping around for his lost shoe, says, "There's not much involved. You could organize the odd job here and there when I have important visitors. Perhaps put in an appearance now and then—you know, the great hunter-author charms the rich provincials."

"I don't know. It's not exactly my cup of tea. I'm more at home with animals."

"Yes, McRory, I get your point. But you have to understand, I'm only trying to keep Sergeant Van Tranh from creating difficulties. Otherwise I can't guarantee your safety in the future." He shrugs. "This can be a very cruel country."

McRory regards him with a smile. He knows that this man is under the thumb of His Excellency; Normandin's future depends on His Excellency's good will. On a sudden whim Normandin can be banished to the backwaters forever, and to prevent that from happening he will use McRory any way he can.

"It's very kind of you, Normandin," he says. "I'm grateful that you're looking out for my best interests. So tell me, what can I do to thank you?"

"I need the skin of that Tigress," he answers promptly. "His Excellency is being difficult about the road project again. He has all sorts of objections—financial, desecrating the land, bowing to tourism—all rot. The real problem is that he lost face during the hunt and he wants to take it out on me." In his agitation, Normandin makes another stab for his missing shoe. Madame Normandin darts a flustered glance at the handsome adventurer, not questioning for a moment that it's his foot doing a flirtatious rub and wiggle. *You say you're more at home with animals,* she thinks, *but that's what you are. An animal. A beautiful, dangerous animal!*

Returning her emotionally overheated glance with a raised eyebrow, McRory wonders if his hostess is ill or having some sort of emotional reaction peculiar to females. He smiles briefly, then returns his gaze to Normandin.

"I read the man somewhat differently," he says. "He doesn't strike me as overly prideful, considering that he possesses incredible power and privilege. In fact he didn't seem to think he'd killed the tiger, and made it clear with his comment about how fast a dead tiger can run. I would say there's more irony in the man than hubris."

"I don't agree. He might not flaunt his position, but there's never a second that he's not aware of it."

"Suppose he just doesn't want the road," McRory says. "It may be that simple."

Normandin shakes his head. "You just don't understand these people, McRory. You're a newcomer and used to British bluntness."

McRory smiles. "It's true we're blunt. But then again, some of us are subtle."

"It's all about honor here," Normandin says, disregarding his comment. "His Excellency's father would never have missed his clear shot at the tiger. His Excellency knows that, and he knows that we know it. We've called attention to his ineptitude simply by being witnesses, and he cannot forgive us for that."

"You told him that he killed the tiger. That might have been a mistake."

"I was only trying to placate him."

"He may have felt you were patronizing him."

Normandin breaks off and shoots a sharp glance at his wife, wondering why she looks so pink and is playing nervously with her silverware.

"Are you all right, my dear?"

"Yes. Perfectly."

"You look a bit under the weather."

"I'm *fine*, Eugene."

Her eyes sweep across McRory very quickly before returning to her lap.

Under the table, things are coming to a head. Raoul, trying to restrain Sangha from venturing out from under the tablecloth, pulls him back by the tail, but Sangha breaks loose and moves forward again, clutching the Administrator's shoe in his mouth. The struggle between the boy and the cub causes Normandin's shoe to rub with considerable force against the high-heeled shoe of Madame Normandin. She jumps slightly in her chair and raises a hand to her mouth. This time both men pretend not to notice her bizarre behavior.

McRory says, "I see a bit of a problem with your request, Normandin."

"Let's hear it, man," he responds with ill-concealed impatience. "All problems are capable of solution when wise men put their heads together."

"Well," McRory says, "here's the thing I don't quite understand. How do you present the man with the skin of a tiger that is still inside it. That strikes me as quite a puzzle."

Madame Normandin stifles a giggle behind her hand.

"You're the hunter," Normandin says, glaring at his wife. "I leave that to you to figure out."

"How long do I have?"

"That's the rub. I have an appointment with His Excellency the day after tomorrow, and I can't go empty-handed."

"Two days? That's impossible. There is no way I can track a cat down in two days. And especially the cat he injured. Do you have any idea what injured animals do?"

"What do they do, McRory. Please don't take offense, but I'm in no mood for riddles."

"They hide where it's hard to find them. And if you do find them, they have grown doubly dangerous. It's called fighting for your life."

"I hate the word impossible," Normandin says heavily. "It's defeatist." His eyes are boiling over with annoyance as he tries, unsuccessfully, to stare down the hunter. "I thought nothing was impossible for an Englishman."

"We lost the American colonies," McRory points out.

Normandin bangs the table with his fist, causing his bemused wife to jump again. Her cheeks have faded from pink to ashen gray. "That remark is impertinent and has nothing to do with the situation we're facing. Come, man, let's be serious for a moment. You're a skillful hunter—a hunter with an international reputation. You can do this, I know you can." He pauses, then adds quietly, with a note of menace, "Otherwise, I may not be able to restrain the Sergeant. He tells me you have acquired an accomplice. Some local girl—"

McRory cuts him off with a chopping motion. "If the Sergeant has something to tell me, let him tell me to my face. I'm not interested in hearing things second-hand."

The activity under the table appears to have taken a turn for the better, unlike the conversation three feet to the north. Raoul has managed to remove the shoe from Sangha's mouth and has placed it directly under his father's shoeless foot. A penitent Sangha, having given up this playful diversion, sits quietly against the boy's lap. But then he makes the slightest move and his little behind presses against the service button on the floor. A bell rings somewhere faraway and a moment later footsteps sound in the hallway. The door to the dining room opens and the butler and one of the houseboys enter.

"Did you ring, Madame?" the butler asks.

Suddenly there is chaos.

Bitzy, seeing his chance, has entered the room through the houseboy's legs. He lunges for the table and dashes under it, barking shrilly. Sangha sees his enemy and he scrambles to get away. He is desperately hanging on to the tablecloth, but Bitzy is all over him now, biting and scratching with the full force of his pent-up fury. He wants his rightful place in the family back, and this is his chance.

Madame Normandin watches in horror. As the tablecloth moves and France's finest porcelain smashes to pieces on the floor, McRory assumes a bland expression, while Normandin buries his face in his hands.

11

Late the following morning Kumal is dozing in his cage, his eyes open just a slit and sometimes fluttering closed. His little head rests on the tail of the old tiger, which has passed from his cage into Kumal's. The tiger cub's nostrils quiver as he sniffs the air. He opens his eyes wide and sits up. A few paces away he sees the outline of a pale upright creature pacing back and forth in the menagerie.

It is the pale man. His friend has come back! Kumal calls out to him, then moves up against the bars and calls out again. His meows are loud and insistent.

He watches as the man turns around and glances at him. He sees the man's eyes widen in recognition. The pale man, his friend, quickly walks up to him and Kumal rubs like a house cat against the bars of the cage. He extends his paws out to the man, trying to catch some part of him to hold.

"Hey, I know you," McRory says. "Fancy finding you again."

He puts his hand inside the cage, reaching for his furry back. Kumal rolls over, the better for the man to rub his belly. He shivers deliciously as he feels the familiar fingers petting him. He starts cooing and stares up at McRory with his round, greenish golden eyes.

"So they brought you here," the pale man says. He sighs as he looks around the dark menagerie, at the manure piling up, the skeletal animals pacing endlessly back and forth in their cages, some of them fixing on him with their feverish sickly eyes.

He continues to rub Kumal and forces himself to speak to the cub in a playful tone.

"Well, little fellow, it's not so bad. Really it isn't. I've seen worse, believe me. At least you've got some company. I can tell that old tiger likes you and you like him." McRory gestures toward the bowl and grins. "Why you even have room service. Not every cub can make that claim."

In the cage next to Kumal's, the old tiger, his head resting on his paws, looks apathetically at the human visitor. He watches as Kumal sniffs McRory's hand repeatedly. Then he begins to lick it.

"You have a long memory for such a little chap, you greedy little thing. I don't know if I have any on me. Wait a minute."

McRory searches in his pocket with one hand as he continues to scratch the cub with his other. He pulls out a honey drop, which he offers to Kumal on the palm of his hand. As McRory watches him lick the sweet eagerly, a hot lump of sadness constricts his throat. He realizes how much he has missed the little cub. What kind of life lies ahead for him in captivity? The hunter does not want to think about it.

"Don't look at me like that, little fellow," he says, continuing to scratch him under his chin. "What was I supposed to do? Put yourself in my place. I couldn't have left you there. You'd have been eaten right away— that is, if you didn't starve to death first. You're not big enough to handle the wild by yourself. You don't know how to hunt, you aren't capable of defending yourself. Don't you see, little chap? I had no choice."

Kumal purrs with pleasure as the man's fingers continue to scratch his chin. When he hears the deep voice of the dark upright creature, though, he shrinks against the side of the cage with a low growl.

"I wouldn't do that if I were you," Zerbino says.

McRory turns around to face the animal tamer. "Are you speaking to me?"

"Even at that age they can take your finger off. They are not domesticated pets."

"I'm not concerned," McRory says mildly.

"Well, maybe you should be. I happen to be an expert in animal behavior, and I've seen the results of carelessness. Please remove your hand from that cage. I won't be put in a position of responsibility for your welfare."

Kumal whimpers as the pale man removes his hand.

"Tell me," he says, "I've heard you keep the skins of your animals when they're dead. Is that true?"

"Sometimes."

"You wouldn't have a tiger hide by any chance, would you? I'm willing to pay dearly for it."

Zerbino studies the handsome and elegant Englishman, whose shiny boots alone are worth a month's box office receipts of his international circus.

"You want a tiger skin?"

"That's right. And I need it quickly."

"May I ask what purpose you would have for a tiger skin?"

"You're free to ask," McRory tells him. "But I'm afraid it's a private matter."

Zerbino nods and smiles his horrible smile. "I see."

He does not like this Englishman with his articulate speech and elegant ways, and is prepared to say so when a voice says, "We can get you a tiger skin. That's no problem at all, my friend."

Saladin has emerged from behind a cage, wringing his hands and bowing

Still taken up with his discovery of the tiger cub, and torn between the cub and his need to deliver a tiger skin to Normandin, McRory fails to notice the surprised look that Zerbino gives his cohort, or the shrug and complicit grin that Saladin gives Zerbino in return. He looks away from Kumal and asks, "Can I see the hide?"

"Of course, of course," Saladin gushes. "When do you need it?"

"Tomorrow. Actually, I can take it off your hands right now if you have it here."

"Tomorrow," Zerbino says. "That's—that's awfully short notice. I'm not sure we can deliver it that quickly." He shoots a look at Saladin.

The magician says, "Tomorrow is no problem, no problem at all. We are always eager to cooperate with gentlemen such as yourself. We will have the hide ready for you to pick up by noon tomorrow. Would that be satisfactory?"

"Perfectly," McRory says. He hesitates, then adds, "It has to be the hide of an adult tiger, you understand."

Saladin nods vigorously and says, "An adult hide, yes, of course." He clears his throat and his eyes slide away from McRory. "It will cost you one thousand piastres, payable in advance."

McRory regards the strange man in his strange costume with curiosity. "One thousand piastres? I don't want the hide finished in gold leaf."

Zerbino laughs and slaps his knee. "That is very amusing. You are a very humorous gentleman." His small dark eyes, however, are not laughing.

"That's the price," Saladin says with a shrug. "I'm not a man who haggles. Take it or leave it. It's up to you. We have many calls for hides."

McRory sneaks a look at Kumal and says casually, "How about throwing in the little one for good measure."

"I'm afraid that is out of the question."

"He's just a cub," McRory says. "What do you want with a little fellow like him?"

"Kumal," Zerbino puts in. "That's his name. We have big plans for him."

"As a future star in our international circus," Saladin adds.

"I'll pay extra for him," McRory says. "Just name your price."

"And what would we show to our customers?" Saladin says, flourishing his hands dramatically. "A circus without a tiger has no business calling itself a circus. It's like an opera without a music score—a mockery. It took us long enough to find Kumal, and as far as we're concerned he's priceless."

McRory nods. "As I said, name your price. Everything has a price."

"You're wasting your time, sir. The cub is not for sale. So to the business at hand—are you prepared to purchase the hide or not? I have plenty of other customers who will buy it if you're not interested. The price, as I said, is one thousand piastres, and that is not negotiable. If that is not satisfactory, I would advise you to take your business elsewhere."

"You drive a hard bargain," McRory says as he takes out his wallet and slowly counts the bills. He looks over at Kumal, whose bright eyes are watching his every move.

"We have a deal," he says with a glance at Zerbino, who seems the less cruel of the two men. "But do me a favor, as a gentleman. Please spend some of this on the little tyke. Feed him well. He happens to be a very good friend of mine."

* * *

The following day, His Excellency sits in the trophy room of his villa, posing for a camera set up on a tripod. He holds a tiger hide across his knees and stares seriously into the camera's eye as the photographer, hidden inside a black cloth, clicks away. The photographer, an aging, bearded man, emerges from under the cloth and regards the young leader with a quizzical stare. "Your Excellency, your father always liked to show the death wound in the picture."

"I am not my father," the young leader says.

"Where is the hole?" says his companion, the former cabaret dancer.

"Never mind that," he says, waving a hand dismissively.

"I want to *know*," she pouts. She leans over the tiger's head and finds a hole under the ear. "Isn't that just amazing? Poor tiger! Poor thing!" She pats the skin tenderly.

"It is amazing," His Excellency says dryly. "Also very meticulous on the part of whomever prepared this for me. Unfortunately, though, the tiger I shot was hit in the other ear."

She looks at him blankly. "I don't understand."

"That's all right," he says wearily. "I didn't expect that you would."

Exasperated both by this farce and by his silly chatty companion, the young man flings the skin to the floor and gets up and leaves the room without another word.

* * *

McRory has returned to Zerbino's circus in a foul mood. He stands close to Zerbino and Saladin, his face rigid with anger. Nai-Rea, close beside him, looks on anxiously. She senses that the usually imperturbable hunter can be dangerous when crossed.

"The hide was supposed to be delivered to me," he says. "I paid for it."

"But the assistant to Monsieur l'Administrateur collected it this morning. He said it was urgent."

"We also understand that you will be reimbursed by Monsieur Normandin," Saladin adds, smiling and nodding repeatedly. "Is that not true?"

McRory disregards him. His eye falls on a raggedly dressed assistant who is sweeping out the old tiger's cage; the cage is empty and the tiger is nowhere to be seen. McRory returns his gaze to Saladin, his blue eyes like ice.

"You are beneath contempt," he says in a voice barely above a whisper. "This was not the arrangement I paid for. I never would have allowed this. Not in a million years."

Saladin's grin slips, but he continues to leer at the hunter. "Come now, Mr. McRory, don't pretend you didn't know where the hide was coming from. Did you think we would be able to conjure a tiger skin out of thin air? Besides, we did that worthless old wretch a favor. We put him out of his misery."

"He didn't have long to go," Zerbino puts in nervously.

McRory notices little Kumal searching and sniffing the air for his old pal. He cries out pitifully, but the assistant grabs him by the scruff of the neck and transfers him to the old tiger's cage, which is more spacious.

"What are you crying about, Kumal?" Zerbino says, flashing his hideous smile. Nai-Rea looks quickly away. "You've just been promoted. You should be pleased with yourself."

Over the cage, the gold sign still reads CAESAR, THE MAN-EATER. This is Kumal's fate, to live his life as a slave for these men, McRory realizes. And it was his decision that brought the cub to this hopeless pass.

He turns to Zerbino and Saladin. "You are both murderers," he says.

"Nonsense," Zerbino replies, looking flustered.

McRory regards Saladin with contempt. "You're suggesting that what you did to that tiger was an act of mercy."

"That is true, sir."

"Well, this is what I would wish for both of you. That you could be out in the jungle without a rifle, at the mercy of animals who might be hungry enough to consider you their next best meal. That's what I would wish for both of you. You deserve nothing less."

"Come, Aidan," Nai-Rea says gently. She takes him by the arm and starts to lead him out, but he cannot tear his eyes away from Kumal. The cub calls out to his pale friend in a series of whimpers, and their eyes meet. The cub cannot understand why his friend is looking at him with that fixed expression, stern and without feeling, and why he does not come to him. He needs the man and he does not come!

Kumal strains toward his friend, his cries growing louder. McRory after a final look at the cub casts his eyes down, grips Nai-Rea's hand and walks slowly away until he is out of Kumal's sight.

12

A month has passed since McRory departed for a trip deep into the jungle with Nai-Rea as his guide. Time, however, has done little to heal his hurt over Kumal. He blames himself for the cub's captivity; he should never have meddled in the animal's affairs. If he had left Kumal in the wild, he might have found a surrogate parent to protect him until he was mature and powerful enough to fend for himself.

"I don't agree," Nai-Rea has told him repeatedly. "If you'd left him in the jungle he would have died, or worse, grown up a man-eater. What is it they say? It's the nature of the beast."

"I suppose," McRory says, but she can hear the doubt in his voice. "Tigers kill men and hunters kill tigers. That seems to be a given, and I've always accepted it as such. But that was before I got to know Kumal. Animals are far from human, but he's taught me that they do have some marked human qualities of compassion and loyalty."

"Tigers are not dogs, Aidan."

"I know that. But they have qualities beyond the killer-survival instinct."

As they discuss this issue, not for the first time, McRory is sitting in the stern of the boat near a small fire where Nai-Rea is preparing tea, while workers pole a long bamboo raft around the rocks and tree stumps that jut out of the water. An enormous statue of Buddha is laid out on the raft and fastened securely with ropes. A smile lights up its face as it stares up through the trees that overhang the river at the vast blue canvas of sky above.

"Remember, Aidan, you're a hunter," Nai-Rea says. "Your job is to protect people from wild animals, the ones that have a history of attacking people. It's important to kill them, and very, very dangerous to pity them."

McRory sits in silence for a moment, then says, "When I lived in Kenya that's exactly what I used to think. Kill or be killed." He smiles at her. "I guess, for me, this thing I'm feeling is a little like religion. First I was a firm believer—kill the buggers before they get you—and now I seem to be becoming a bit of a doubter."

"Hunting is a noble occupation, you know. You mustn't ever lose sight of that. You're like the policeman of the jungle, keeping law and order and protecting the citizens."

"I've never much liked policemen," he says. "And as for noble occupation, what's better than showing the treasures of your country to people who have a chance to see them? That sounds like a noble occupation to me."

Nai-Rea reaches out and ruffles his hair. "I think you just changed the subject."

"But don't you agree?"

"Well, my father agrees," she answers with a sly smile. "Especially if you give him the money."

Underneath her banter, McRory can hear the reproach in her words, and he feels a need to defend himself. "The thing is, nobody sees the statues here— apart from a few bats they are wasted. It's as though they don't exist."

"Yes, but the point is, they do exist. It's like the old riddle. If a tree falls in the forest and there's no one to hear it, has it made a sound? Well, of course it has. I don't need to be a philosopher to know that. And it's the same way with the statues. We may not see them but we know they're there. Do you need to see God to know He exists?"

"I don't follow your line of thought," he says. "My God isn't left to decay in the jungle. He lives a full and active life in my heart."

"The jungle is their home, Aidan. This is where the statues live, this is their home, and it's been their home for thousands of years."

"It's also where the tigers live," he counters. "They have been here longer than any stone Buddha, and yet you don't mind my hunting them."

"I stated my reasons, whether you accept them or not. They come to kill us in our fields. They have no regard for human life. What do the statues do? They add beauty and history to the land. They destroy nothing."

She hesitates, fighting to get a grip on her growing anger. Her hand shakes as she pours tea.

"I think I've offended you deeply," he says at last, to break the silence. "If I have, I apologize. That wasn't my intention."

She turns to him, her eyes red-rimmed with emotion. "Do you remember the young man who gave you this?" With the point of her finger, she reaches out and touches the necklace he is wearing around his neck. "The boy who lost his leg to a tiger?"

"I remember."

"He is my brother," Nai-Rea says.

McRory stares at her, at a loss for words.

* * *

Chaos once again visits the Normandin household. The lap dog, Bitzy, still struggling to regain what he considers his rightful place in the family as number one animal, is barking loudly and incessantly at the shelf in Raoul's bedroom. Above his small, furious form the shelf sags dangerously under the weight of Sangha, who has grown much larger on a diet of French food and easy domesticity. For a moment there is a standoff in the continuing power struggle between dog and tiger, punctuated by Bitzy's barks and Sangha's growls. Even though he has grown larger and stronger, Sangha is timid by nature and tries to avoid confrontation at all costs. His instinct now is to find a way to become invisible among the stuffed animals. As Bitzy's barks increase in both intensity and duration, it is clear to a neutral observer—to Raoul, say—that Bitzy is unaware of the reversal in power that has occurred between him and Sangha. It must also be said that Sangha is unaware of it, even though he has grown bigger, while the dog has remained tiny.

Bitzy jumps and lets out an ear-splitting howl, which in translation says: "Get out of my master's room and stay out. This is *my* domain!"

At that moment, the shelf collapses with a thunderous crash. In the kitchen—too distant for the sound to travel—the butler is putting the finishing touches on a breakfast tray for Madame Normandin. He fusses with the arrangement of wildflowers in a crystal vase, and as he is about to exit the kitchen the swinging door hits him flush in the face. He is thrown backwards, the tray flying out of his hands, food splattering everywhere. Sangha bursts into the kitchen at full speed, with Bitzy, wild with rage, hot on his heels.

Sangha jumps over the terrified butler, still lying on the floor, and takes off for the hallway. Running full out, he misses the turn and crashes into a coat stand that topples over, just missing Bitzy only strides behind him. Sangha, howling with fear, manages to extricate himself from the collection of colonial helmets, hats and umbrellas scattered about, and escapes just in time to avoid his fierce assailant. Off they go again, the black-and-orange streak that is a clearly frightened Sangha and a small black ball of determined canine rage.

In the Administrator's office, Normandin, in his official costume, including epaulets, is receiving a delegation of Annamese dignitaries dressed in short pants and top hats. The pointer he holds in his pudgy hand traces the winding road on a large relief map. He tries to ignore the commotion he hears in some other part of the house and raises his voice to speak over it.

"Soon," he thunders, "the sacred statues, our pride and joy, will no longer need to leave their temples and migrate to Paris, London and other centers of culture...."

One of the dignitaries looks up, concerned by the commotion and barking. He tries to catch Normandin's eye, but the Administrator presses on.

"Thanks to this road, we will be able to keep our statues here where they belong," he shouts, "and why is that, you may be asking yourselves? The answer is both simple and compelling. Because those Parisians seeking culture—as well as Englishmen and Americans and—and others—will come to the temples. As tourism increases, our economy will———"

Normandin gets no further.

"Good God!" screams one of the dignitaries, jumping up onto his chair.

The young tiger, howling and with teeth bared, bursts into the room, followed by the lapdog, foam collecting around the corners of his mouth. Sangha rams into the stools supporting the map, knocking it over, then he skids on a rug. Many of the dignitaries—the road question all but forgotten—manage to slip out the door; the less intrepid, however, are too stunned and terrified to move. The plaster-bust "Marianne," the symbol of the French Republic, tilts on its pedestal, then topples over onto a huge aquarium, which explodes. Water, seaweed and shells splatter on the floor at the feet of the remaining members of the delegation. One of the dignitaries, a very old man with an impressive mane of wavy white hair, contemplates his oversized sandal, which is now soaked with water. He removes a wiggling goldfish from under his big toe.

Normandin retrieves the moist map and clutching it in two hands, mumbles, "My son's pet. Grown rather large, I'm afraid. It's all in fun—but—yes, out of hand, no question about it. Must make some other arrangements. Yes—as I was saying, the statues will never again have to be exported. They belong to this land, as part of our great heritage, and here they will stay...."

Sangha and Bitzy, racing on after leaving the Administrator's office in partial ruin, have entered the laundry room at the end of the hallway. Sangha quickly realizes that he's faced with a dead end. He is cornered with no possible means of escape. He squeezes himself under the sink, and trembling all over, curls up into a big ball of fur. Facing him, Bitzy moves in to attack with a series of fearful yaps.

It is at that precise instant that the balance of power between dog and tiger shifts forever. In his fear, Sangha lashes out with his paw, and as Bitzy, with a howl of surprise and pain, drops to the floor, the tiger lashes out again. This time there is no response from the dog beyond a weak whimper.

Madame Normandin, clad in a white silk bathrobe, comes running down the hallway and freezes at the door of the laundry room. Her hand flies to her mouth and she screams. Her beloved lapdog has a small rip in his stomach from which blood is leaking in slow drops. He looks up at her with the saddest expression imaginable. Sangha, too, stares at her as he shakes feverishly. There is stark terror in his eyes. He senses that he has done something unforgivable in the woman's eyes.

"Oh my God! *My God!*" she wails. "You killed him! You killed my Bitzy!"

The lapdog, mauled but very much alive, lets out a few bleats of anguish.

A moment later, Sangha is surrounded. He is confronted by brooms, rakes and pitchforks in the hands of the staff, all pointing at him, and the faces behind the implements are cruel. He knows that these upright creatures are very angry and very frightened, and he also knows that there is nothing he can do about it. He attacked the dog. It didn't matter that the dog attacked him first, and had been doing so at every opportunity from the day the boy adopted him. He didn't want to harm the dog, he'd had no intention to strike out at him, but then it just happened. It was as though his paw had taken on a life of its own, and, sensing danger, had acted independently of the rest of him. And worst of all, while he was battering Bitzy, it had seemed natural and right.

Confronted by the angry kitchen staff, Sangha backs up over the vestibule tiling, hoping to find some way to get free. The butler opens and closes an umbrella under his nose as both a weapon and a shield. The cook armors himself with a pot cover and points his meat cleaver at Sangha, gladiator-style. Slowly, the tiger is driven backwards through the front door of the residence. They then back him up still farther, until he finds himself inside a wooden chamber at the level of the front steps. A constable, who was called to the house, quickly closes the door. The chamber is actually the inside of a horse-drawn paddy wagon, which had been backed up to the front steps of the Normandin house. The word POLICE is painted on the side in white block letters. After a brief conversation with Madame Normandin, the constable climbs up to the driver's seat and takes the reins.

Inside the wagon, Sangha stands up on his hind legs, and through the bars of the window in back he can see the face of the boy as he comes running to the wagon.

The boy is his friend. The boy is crying and will save him. He puts his hand through the bars to pet his tiger.

"They can't take you from me," he sobs. "It's not fair, Sangha. It's just not fair."

Sangha licks the child's hand. He loves the boy, Raoul, and he cannot bear to see him hurt and sad.

"You're mine," Raoul says. "They have no right to take you away. I hate them!"

Madame Normandin, clutching the moaning Bitzy to her bosom, yanks her son away from the wagon.

"Raoul, you don't hate anyone and you mustn't say such a nasty thing. Come away now. You're to have nothing more to do with that monster."

"He was only playing," the boy wails. "He didn't mean to hurt Bitzy. They play all the time and Bitzy usually starts it. It wasn't Sangha's fault."

"Nonsense," she says, her voice shrill with hysteria. "Look at the size of him, look how he's grown. He's a tiger now, Raoul, not a little plaything anymore. He has a taste for blood now." She thrusts Bitzy in front of the boy. "Look what he did to my poor puppy."

Raoul turns back to the tiger. "I don't care how big he gets. He's Sangha. He'll always be Sangha." Tears are flowing down his cheeks.

The constable cracks a whip and the horses pull the wagon over the cobblestone path. Raoul watches from the steps as Sangha, behind bars, is taken away like a dangerous criminal. The tiger watches through the bars of the wagon as the outline of his weeping friend, his one real friend in the world, grows ever smaller in the fading light of evening.

Raoul turns to his mother, his fists clenched. "You had no right to send him away. Sangha belongs to me."

"Excuse me, my dear boy, but as your mother I have every right. You have none. Just look what he did to poor Bitzy."

"He's hardly bleeding, Mother."

"That's not the point. He tried to kill my dog and one day he will be a killer. He may have been a cute little cub at one time, but tigers grow up to be savages. It's built into them. It's their nature."

Raoul regards his mother, the cold questioning light of adulthood in his gaze. "I'll never forgive you for this," he says. "Never…"

* * *

The paddy wagon stops in the courtyard of His Excellency's villa, and the constable steps down to greet the majordomo. "I'm in charge of the menagerie," the majordomo says with all the haughtiness of his rank and position. "I understand you have brought a gift for His Excellency."

"Yes, a gift from Monsieur l'Administrateur, in the name of France."

"Ah yes. Please follow me."

The palace's underground corridors echo with angry roars and growls. Sets of eyes shine feverishly in the dark, behind bars. Preceded by the majordomo carrying a torch, the constable pulls the young tiger behind him on the end of a long iron chain; the sound of their footsteps bounce off the damp stone vaults. The dim light reveals a fresco; the mosaic pictures a Roman arena where lions and bears are engaged in a fight to the death.

Terrified, Sangha looks at the cages lined up on either side of him. He can vaguely make out the shadows of the creatures inside. He refuses to move forward, his claws scrape the ground. The majordomo points at the long, wet trail Sangha has left behind him and regards the constable skeptically. "Pissing on himself. This half-grown animal seems scared to death. He'll need a lot of training."

The constable shrugs and says nothing. He has done his duty and has no further interest in the outcome.

"Is he really as savage as the Administrator says? Frankly, I don't see any signs of it."

The constable glances around at the menagerie's occupants, as ill at ease as his prisoner.

"You wouldn't ask if you'd seen what he did to the Administrator's dog."

"Ripped him up, did he?"

"It was a terrible sight."

"Of course that's just a dog," the majordomo says as he studies the tiger curiously. "We have bigger things in mind for him."

PART TWO

13

Six months have passed. In the lives of tigers, six months is many human years, and the physical growth of a tiger in its first year is remarkable. The two brothers, Kumal and Sangha, although still young and unsettled in their minds, have grown into impressive adult specimens of tigerhood. They both have only dim recollections of their mother—there are moments when they miss her, others when they forget her altogether. They also have dim recollections of each other, sometimes feeling the loss and sadness of something they cannot quite place.

Kumal is caught in a constant struggle between his natural aggressive instincts and a growing timidity. He senses that his own survival is at stake, and if he doesn't obey the upright creatures with their whips and chains and hoops and sudden bolts of fire he will go the way of the old tiger. He resents being caged and having to perform, and his captors realize that. Their strategy is to grind the danger out of his system with constant training and, if necessary, occasional beatings and food deprivation. But the rage against them is still there; it is simply buried deep inside where they cannot see it.

"Jump, Kumal! Jump!"

Across from him, Zerbino, dressed in his tight, bright red tamer's costume, holds up a flaming hoop.

"Jump, there's nothing to it. Jump—you can do it. *Jump!*"

Flames reflect in Kumal's eyes. He growls softly and arches his back. He wants no part of the heat or the flame, and at the same time he knows that eventually the upright creatures will break him down and get their way.

"You're going to go through it," Zerbino implores. "Once you do it, you'll be fine. The next time will be easy. You'll see."

Sitting on a stool, Kumal stares at the circle of fire. He continues to growl low in his throat, then turns his head away and stares directly at the animal tamer, his greenish-golden eyes gleaming in the flames. His intense stare unnerves even the experienced Zerbino. He senses that Kumal is not like the usual run of tigers he has trained.

He cracks his whip. He is uncomfortable with the audience made up of his wife, Saladin and the assistants. He is aware that Saladin thinks he is far too soft on the tiger, that he is slow in taming him, perhaps over fearful. Even his wife has grown impatient with him; she has questioned his manhood and hinted that he may be losing his touch.

"Come on, Kumal," he urges. "Jump, *jump…*"

The young tiger stubbornly refuses.

"You're babying the animal," Saladin explodes. "This is getting us nowhere.'

He approaches Kumal, armed with a pitchfork, and jabs at him.

"Leave him to me," Zerbino says. "You know nothing about the art of taming wild beasts. Those strong-arm tactics aren't going to work—not with this tiger."

"How can you say that if you don't try?"

"I know what I'm doing, Saladin. Stay out of it."

Zerbino cracks his whip again and Kumal steps down from the stool. He walks around the hoop and sits on the stool on the other side. He then sits up and begs, performing all the circus tricks he has learned thus far, hoping to satisfy the upright creatures and so to avoid the hoop of fire.

"You stupid animal, jump! You know how to do it. Don't strain my patience." Zerbino is starting to feel humiliated.

Saladin laughs contemptuously. "How pathetic," he says. "Those are stunts worthy of a cub. This animal is full-grown and he's learned nothing. Audiences will boo him off the stage." He exchanges a look with Madame Zerbino, who smiles back conspiratorially.

Zerbino is aware of the interchange and it enrages him. He turns angrily to the tiger. Kumal guards his head against the whip with a raised paw. He hates this man, but it is the other man who shoots fire from his mouth whom he truly fears.

"You'll never manage it," Saladin says. "You have no control over the animal."

He stands and rummages inside his jacket.

"What are you doing?" Zerbino says.

"It's time to try new tactics," Saladin replies. "You've made it too easy for him, Zerbino. The tiger is living off us and giving us nothing in return. We need to put some fright in him." He draws a pistol and holds it under Kumal's nose. He pulls the trigger and the blank cartridge explodes in a cloud of smoke. The sound unleashes a sudden fury in Kumal; he leaps down into the ring, whirls around, roars at the top of his lungs and charges like lightning at Saladin.

"How dare you, you stupid beast!" the magician screams. He snatches a stool and Kumal rushes into the metal legs. Continuing to fend off the enraged animal with the stool, Saladin says, "Once and for all, it's time you learned who is your master."

"Let me," Zerbino puts in nervously. "You're not a tamer—you have no patience, no understanding of his ways. I can do this."

He is furious at being usurped, but Saladin continues to ignore him. He gestures to the assistants. "Come on, all of you. We're going to teach this beast a lesson he won't soon forget. No more coddling him."

The assistants, over Zerbino's protestations, surge forward; they help Saladin back Kumal up against the bars. The tiger snarls and bares his fangs as a noose is tightened around his neck. An assistant who has remained outside the cage grabs the rope and pulls hard on it. Kumal is being strangled, his head crushed against the bars. His tongue is hanging out.

"Now you're going to learn some manners." Saladin leers at the tiger, hatred glittering from his black eyes.

At his command, the assistants grab their whips, ready to use them if necessary. Saladin takes his pitchfork and hits the tiger on his flanks with the handle. Zerbino looks on in grim silence. As an experienced tiger tamer he knows that although Saladin may get some grudging cooperation by using torture tactics, he is also making a mortal enemy of the tiger, and one day when Saladin's back is turned....

The sounds of Kumal's punishment, his rage-engorged roars, the men yelling—this cacophony of sounds stirs up the other animals. A bear begins to shake the bars of his cage; two wolves run back and forth in their cages, howling; monkeys leap wildly from perch to perch, chattering hysterically. Chaos reigns in all the cages.

Twenty minutes later, Kumal is finally subdued. He sits on the stool in sullen silence, head down and avoiding eye contact. Saladin, with a meaningful glance at Zerbino, says, "You see what can be done if you don't cater to the animal? Now we'll see the effects of my brand of taming."

He takes a big gulp of gasoline, and, holding a torch, blows out a long line of fire. He uses the fire to set his hoop ablaze, then kneels and shows Kumal the circle of fire. He cracks a whip and says, "Now, jump, Kumal, *jump*..."

Beaten and struggling against his aversion to fire, Kumal finally leaps and passes through the flames, and lands on the stool on the opposite side.

"There you go," Saladin exults. "Now that wasn't so hard, was it? I knew you had it in you."

Zerbino, as defeated as the tiger, raises the trap door of the tunnel that leads to the menagerie. The man is an absolute fool, he thinks. He doesn't realize that he has made a very dangerous and implacable enemy. One day he is going to pay.... He watches as Kumal rushes into the trap door, hunkering down inside. Hunched over, his tail between his legs, he crosses through the wild animal tunnel. He sees the cage, his refuge, his pitiful home, open before him and jumps inside. He limps over and huddles in the darkest corner and slowly lies down, avoiding his painful flank. He stares dully into the distance.

Saladin meets with Zerbino and Madame Zerbino later in the office. He says triumphantly, "The tiger is finally ready to perform master stunts in front of an audience. We have broken him successfully." He meets the gaze of Madame Zerbino, who beams at him with undisguised admiration. Zerbino says nothing. Saladin regards him with a smile and cannot resist adding, "To you, tigers are special animals. But the truth is, they are just animals. And what do you do with animals? You break them with force and your superior human intellect."

Zerbino shakes his head, turns and strides out of the room.

* * *

Two weeks later, a black limousine, followed by a swarm of half-naked children, clatters over potholes and stops in the village square in front of the spot where the Zerbino family circus has set up its tent. A turbaned chauffeur holds the back door open and the majordomo steps out. He takes in the scene with a haughty glance and walks over to a circus poster entitled BLOODY KUMAL, THE KILLER OF THE MEKONG. It shows the tiger holding the remains of his unfortunate—and entirely fictitious—tamer in his jaws.

Zerbino and Saladin walk over to the automobile, drawn by its elegance.

"Is your tiger as ferocious as advertised?" the major-domo asks.

Saladin tries to smile pleasantly but only manages a supercilious leer. "Why don't you test him, sir? If you have a spare arm or leg, I'll gladly give you the key to his cage."

The majordomo stares coldly at the clownishly dressed man with his garish makeup. "My master is mounting a festival," he says. "It is to be organized exactly as it was in the time of his late father. Have you heard of these ceremonies?"

"Of course," Zerbino answers. "Everyone has." Suddenly concerned, he adds, "What kind of animal would ours be up against?"

"A savage one," the majordomo replies. "We have the best fighting beast in captivity—the best I've ever seen. We want an opponent that's worthy of him."

Zerbino knows that Saladin is going to accept the offer. For the sake of his remaining pride he wants to appear as the man who makes the decisions.

"A special beast means a special price," he says quickly. "Five thousand piastres."

The majordomo regards him, an eyebrow raised. "That's a lot of money," he says.

"Well, ours is a lot of tiger," Saladin puts in.

The majordomo hesitates, then nods curtly.

"He had better be worth it," he says.

"He is," Saladin says.

"You do not want to disappoint His Excellency." There is an undercurrent of warning in the major-domo's words.

"Believe me, you're getting a bargain. Our tiger will give yours his money's worth. Let us know when to stop feeding him. He fights best when he's very hungry."

* * *

That same afternoon, back at the palace, the major-domo holds out a large case covered with old leather. His Excellency nods and opens the jewel box. His companion, the former French cabaret dancer, is awestruck at the sight of a splendid necklace set with huge diamonds and precious stones.

"Are they real?" she whispers.

His Excellency smiles at her with tolerant amusement. "Of course they're real. Everything about my father was real—if rather overdone for modern tastes."

"And will the tiger fight be arranged just as it was in your father's day?"

"Precisely. In every detail," he answers. "The French want to show the people that everything is the same as it used to be. That time has stood still all these years."

"Isn't that just wonderful?" Her smile is bright and yet curiously vacant.

"Isn't what wonderful."

"That they have such respect for their traditions."

"They only want to show that everything is the same in order to hide the fact that everything is different. Time does not stand still. It can't, anymore than gravity can be removed from the earth. They patronize me with their admiration so they can corner me after the ceremony into signing the contract for their damn road."

His soft, youthful face is pinched with anger.

"But why are you against the road?" she asks. "I just don't understand. What's wrong with it?"

"The road represents progress of a kind, I grant that. We can attract tourists to our land to gape at our treasures, and that will put money into the national treasury. That's progress—as I said, of a kind." He regards her seriously. "I know why you came here all the way from France." He smiles. "Certainly not for the climate. Or my good looks."

She darts a fearful look at him. "What do you mean?"

"Normandin is behind it—behind you. No one fooled me from the beginning, but I accepted your company. I am a very lonely man, and your bright chatter is diverting."

"I think you're reading way too much into things."

He waves a hand to silence her. "Don't worry," he says. "You've accomplished your mission. I will tell them you did everything in your power to persuade me the road should be built."

The former dancer is struck dumb by his candor. Her mission has clearly failed. His Excellency hands the necklace to the majordomo with a sigh.

"Make sure the tiger wears this necklace for the contest."

"Why would you put a necklace on a tiger," the cabaret singer asks.

"It's a royal tradition," he says wearily. "I'm simply following in the footsteps of my father."

* * *

On a sudden whim, the youthful potentate decides to visit the menagerie that has been in the royal family for many generations. It is his first visit since he was a small boy. Preceded by the majordomo and servants bearing torches (the former cabaret dancer unceremoniously left behind), he enters the labyrinth and looks around. A water buffalo charges at the bars of his cage and emits a deep and deafening bellow, causing a servant to step quickly to the side in order to dodge the animal's horns, which are rigged with spiked steel extensions.

"Why do we keep them all?" His Excellency asks. "What's the point of it? They're rotting away in here. What good are they?"

"They were your father's," the majordomo answers as though that explains everything.

"We should get rid of them."

"They are dangerous, Your Excellency. We can't just turn them loose. They've been bred to kill."

"Give them to a zoo then."

The majordomo hesitates before saying, "This is the only zoo in the entire country."

"There is one in Saigon."

"I will look into it."

His Excellency, having stated his position, is no longer listening. He watches a vulture watch him as he passes by. Wrapped around his perch, the talons of the bird of prey glow with a murderous glint; they are fitted with razor-sharp metal claws. In the next cage crocodiles snap their cavernous jaws.

"For countless generations your family has maintained this menagerie," the majordomo explains. "It is a tradition. A tradition, I should add, that the people cherish."

His Excellency nods but says nothing. He concedes in his own mind an unwelcome element of truth in the older man's words, and he recognizes, with sadness and resignation, the eternal difficulty faced by a modern ruler of a time-bound people. It is his lot in life to try to change the nearly unchangeable, and it is one that he does not cherish.

He arrives in front of a cage that is more spacious than the others. He stops and stares inside. A young adult tiger is pacing nervously in his iron prison, muscles rippling beneath his orange-and-black coat. Every movement suggests to the young leader a sense of savagery.

He examines the tiger up close and then turns to the majordomo. "Was he born ferocious?"

"He was a very shy animal when he arrived here—full of fear. He had a difficult period of adjustment. But it's always fear that makes us into killers."

On the tiger's neck, reflecting the fire of the torchlight, His Excellency observes the diamond necklace.

"Why do we call him Sangha?" he asks the majordomo.

"The Administrator's child named him. He had him as a pet."

"A pet." His Excellency looks thoughtful. "How interesting." He continues to observe the tiger. "This Sangha—he doesn't look like a killer to me."

"Believe me, he is." The majordomo clears his throat. "Naturally if Your Excellency would like the tiger renamed, he will be called whatever you wish."

The young potentate sighs. "Ah yes. Everything is always as His Excellency wishes." He moves even closer to the cage. "Bring me a chair and then please leave me."

At a sign from the majordomo, a Louis Quinze chair is brought in. The majordomo remains for a moment, hesitant to leave his master alone in the menagerie.

"Your Excellency—as I told you, he is very dangerous."

"Leave me."

Reluctantly, the majordomo departs. His Excellency continues to contemplate the wild animal.

"You're in a cage, Sangha, an unyielding cage, and we have that in common. My cage, too, is unyielding. What am I to do? My own majordomo thinks I can't be trusted to stay clear of a caged tiger. What about you, Sangha? Do you find me stupid—stupid and useless? The French do. To them I'm a perfect fool. They even try to buy me with lovely showgirls and the skin of tigers I haven't killed and promises they can never keep. Yes—to them I'm a perfect fool."

The tiger studies the man curiously with his phosphorescent eyes. He is not used to upright creatures speaking to him in a voice as gentle as a soft breeze.

"Do you remember your father, Sangha? Was he a great lord of the jungle? Mine was. Did all the other creatures shrink in his shadow? That's how it was with mine…and was yours disappointed in his son? Did he wish he'd had one in his image?"

The beast and the man stare at each other. Sangha's head is tilted to the side. He is confused by this man's stream of talk and his soft sad eyes.

"No. I'm sure your father was not that way. I'm sure he was proud of you."

Suddenly something in Sangha snaps. He fakes a charge, and roars in His Excellency's face. The young potentate wipes his face calmly with a silk handkerchief. He leans toward the tiger until his face feels the cold iron of the bars. The man and the tiger are caught in intense eye contact.

"So you, too, think that one must be cruel in this world. That one must be cruel to gain respect. Is that your view of life, Sangha? How sad. How very sad."

Sangha remains motionless as he stares fixedly, with luminous eyes, at this strange soft-spoken man.

14

Later that day, Normandin, his wife and their son Raoul arrive at His Excellency's estate and head toward the arena adjacent to His Excellency's magnificent palace. Behind the arena is the riding stable, where for generations the royal family has bred Arabian stallions. The palace grounds have been raked and groomed to perfection for the big event—the battle of the killer tigers. There is a hum of excitement in the air.

As the Administrator waves to local dignitaries, calling out an occasional name as befits his political gifts, he is carrying on a continuing argument with Madame Normandin in reproving tones.

"Your attitude is most unpleasant, Mathilde."

"But why do I have to be here? Why does it matter? This is simply bestial and I'd rather not have any part of it."

He nods to the mayor of an adjoining village, then says, "Make one last effort today and I won't ask another thing of you. I think we've got him on the hook. He's promised to sign the construction agreement at the end of the ceremony, and once his name is on the dotted line...." Normandin heaves a great sigh of relief and hugs his leather briefcase to his bosom.

"You call this a ceremony," she says tensely. "I call it slaughter, pure and simple."

"It is a sport, my dear. The sport of kings."

"The sport of men who are still boys at heart, killing beasts instead of tearing the wings off bees."

The Administrator snorts derisively. "What rot. You are about to witness a great tradition. I would appreciate a show of enthusiasm."

"If I faint at the first sight of blood, Eugene, don't say I didn't warn you.'

"If I were you, I'd get used to this sort of thing, because if I'm appointed consul to Madrid, as we hope, you will have to attend bullfights every Sunday. As my loyal wife it will be expected of you."

"How ghastly."

The Normandins take their seats in the arena, and the Administrator immediately opens his briefcase and rifles through the pages of the agreement. "Every 'T' is crossed, every 'I' dotted," he tells his wife excitedly. "I think that any objections His Excellency might bring up have been anticipated."

His wife nods, but her attention is riveted on the center of the stands where a canopy has been set up. In its shade, a gilded chair awaits the arrival of His Excellency. She thinks of the cabaret dancer with distaste. A cheap and obvious woman, and a transparent ploy to try and sway His Excellency into accepting the construction of a road through his royal property and into the heart of the jungle. Eugene should have thought his strategy through more carefully. One dinner conversation with His Excellency, she thinks, and I could secure his promise to build the damn road and we would be on our way to Europe.

Raoul breaks in on her thoughts. "I'm not sure I like the idea of a tiger fight," he whines. His youthful forehead is creased with a worried frown. "One of them may die."

"Apparently that's the point," she says. "Talk to your father about it. He's the expert on this sort of thing."

"What worries me is, what if one of the tigers is Sangha? I dreamed that it was him, Mother, and that he got all torn up and was bleeding—"

"Oh stop sniveling," she cuts in sharply. "Of course it won't be your tiger. What an absurd idea."

"I don't think it's absurd at all." The boy glares at her stubbornly. "There can't be that many young tigers in captivity."

"Take it up with your father." She runs the back of her hand across her forehead in a gesture that manages to be both weary and theatrical. "You're giving me a pounding headache."

A moment later, free of Raoul's questions and concerns, her attention shifts to Aidan McRory as he makes his way through the crowd. He looks preoccupied and his eyes are focused on the ring. Close by his side is a beautiful native woman. She is simply but tastefully dressed in a tight silk dress and moves with a proud grace.

Madame Normandin taps her husband on the arm, and reluctantly he looks up from his documents.

"Yes, my dear."

"That woman with McRory…"

"What about her?" He peers at her nearsightedly.

"She's a native."

"So? If you want my opinion, McRory is rather native himself."

"You said he was only interested in statues. Obviously he has other interests."

Normandin continues to stare, a smirk playing on his full lips. "Indeed. I'd like to keep a statue like that one for our provincial museums."

Madame Normandin shoots daggers at Nai-Rea. "I just don't understand what he sees in her. I thought he had better taste. It's very disappointing."

"She's a good-looking woman, Mathilde."

"She is cheap," Madame Normandin snaps. "Cheap and obvious. Just the way you men like them."

McRory, spotting the Normandins, nods and smiles, but deliberately chooses seats too far away for conversation. He is aware that the local gossip is focused on the two of them, and he does not plan to respond to innuendoes and loaded questions.

"I wish they wouldn't stare at me, Aidan. I'm not some exotic zoo animal."

"Why shouldn't they stare at you? I would—in fact I do. I applaud their taste."

"I can read their minds. They don't think you should have brought your native girl to this fancy outing. Bad taste—the worst of all sins in their eyes."

"You're not my native girl," McRory tells her. "You're my girl. If they have a problem, it's theirs, not ours. They just have to get over it."

"They'll never get used to the likes of me, Aidan. They're European."

He slips his arm around her, relishing the attention, unlike her. With his hunter's eye for detail, he inspects the center of the arena and the circular fighting pit that has been set up with golden globes on long spikes, which bear the image of His Excellency. McRory suddenly leans forward, his attention drawn to a man wearing silver-encrusted boots. He has just entered the ring and is checking the strength of the bars. When the man turns around, facing the shaded side of the stands, McRory recognizes him as Zerbino, the tiger tamer.

"No," he says under his breath. "*No.*" He grips Nai-Rea's hand as he jumps up. "I'll be right back," he says. "Don't move."

She nods, not considering questioning him; she was brought up not to question men. She watches as he moves quickly through the crowd toward the exit.

The circus van is parked among the service buildings behind the arena, hidden from the curious eyes of spectators. McRory appears suddenly and rushes up to the cage where Kumal is dozing. He stares at the young tiger, now full grown, and shakes his head.

149

"So...it *is* you. That's what I was afraid of. I'm so sorry."

Aroused by the voice, familiar enough to worm its way through his dreams, Kumal's eyes slowly open.

"Don't you recognize me? I'm not the one who's changed, you have. You're all grown up now—a handsome lad."

McRory removes a honey drop from his safari jacket and tosses it in the cage.

With a vacant look, the tiger watches the honey drop roll under his snout. He does not pick it up. McRory continues to stare at him intensely, hoping for some sign of recognition.

A voice rings out behind him.

"Looking for another tiger skin? That one's not for sale.'

McRory turns around to face Zerbino and Saladin. "But its skin soon will be," he says.

"Depends on the fight he has in him," Saladin says. "If he quits, where would you like the hole in his ear? We always aim to please the customer."

McRory regards the two men, his mouth a thin line of anger. "Do you know what you're doing?" he says, speaking softly to control his anger, which he knows from experience can turn murderous if provoked. "Do you have any idea? I understand that His Excellency's tiger is a wild beast. This is an overgrown poodle, trained to sit up and beg. I don't care how large he is, he'll be torn to pieces."

Zerbino spits on the ground between them. "You've got no right to lecture us. Who do you think you are, God? So one tiger will die—that hardly qualifies as a tragedy. Every penny we earn from this contest will be spent on keeping the rest of our animals alive. You of all people have no right to talk. You're the hunter, not us! You're the one who gets rich by killing dumb beasts."

"I believe in fair fights," McRory says. "This is not meant to be a slaughterhouse."

Saladin throws back his head and laughs. "What a hypocrite you are, Mr. McRory. You believe in slaughter for profit. A fair fight, you say? Who has the rifle, you or the tiger?"

A bird suddenly flies into Kumal's cage and lands a few inches from the tiger's snout and begins pecking away at the wooden floor. The three men approach the cage, and, while their attention is diverted by the bird, McRory removes the key from the lock of the cage and slips it in his pocket. He backs away. "As I said, gentlemen, I believe in fair fights between animals of equal abilities. I'm not going to let this happen."

"Give us the key, you imbecile," Saladin warns, first clenched as he advances on McRory.

"I'll buy him. I'll match what they paid for him. Just name the price."

"You couldn't afford it," Saladin says. "Give me the key! Don't make things hard on yourself."

He raises his hand, and three assistants start to close in on McRory. He backs up against the cage and searches for Kumal's eyes as if seeking his help. Kumal raises his head and looks directly into the hunter's eyes, but his expression is flat and distant. There is still no light of recognition. Slowly and deliberately the animal turns around and shows McRory his hindquarters.

* * *

In the arena, the brass band begins to play. Dressed in kilts and the frogged jackets of Bengal Lancers, the musicians have struck up the triumphant sounds of a bullfight paso doble. Following a protracted drumroll, the majordomo nods discreetly to his master. His Excellency raises his hand to give the signal, then he freezes. He stares at McRory, whose clothing is spattered with mud as he rejoins Nai-Rea. The hunter whispers urgently into Nai-Rea's ear, then takes her by the hand and leaves the arena in full view of everyone.

His Excellency's hand remains raised as he continues to stare after McRory. He is clearly disconcerted, but finally his hand comes down in the signal to proceed. A gong rings out in a long, sustained note.

In the tunnel leading to the arena, Sangha is trembling with excitement. His heart is racing, his blood is boiling with anticipation: he is ready for the kind of action that has been bred into him these past months. When the bars roll up before him he sprints out of the tunnel and bursts into the fighting pit. His tail up, he crosses to the other end, his movements slinky and lethal. The sight of the ferocious beast with the diamond necklace sends a delicious thrill of anticipation through the crowd. With a throaty growl, Sangha flings himself savagely against the bars. The metal seams creak from stress and the solidly anchored bars wobble. One of the golden globes that is hung on the fighting pit is shaken loose and falls to the ground.

In the bleachers, Raoul suddenly jumps to his feet. "It's Sangha! It's Sangha!" He grabs his father by the sleeve of his jacket. "It's Sangha, Father. Just look!"

Normandin and his wife exchange a glance.

"But how could that be?" Normandin says, turning to his son. "You know very well we sent him to the zoo in Saigon."

"That's right," Madame Normandin adds quickly. "You're just imagining things, Raoul. All adult tigers look alike."

"He is hundreds of miles away," Normandin says.

"No he isn't," the boy shouts. "He's right down there. I would know him anywhere." Raoul begins to cry. "Why is he out there anyway? I don't want him to get hurt!"

Normandin glances at his wife with concern, not knowing how to proceed.

She raises a finger to her lips and shakes her head. "There has to be a good explanation. That tiger cub you had—Sangha—was sent to a zoo. We made all the arrangements. This is another tiger."

"*It is Sangha,*" Raoul wails.

The tiger continues to pace back and forth in the pit, a picture of pent-up power. He takes possession of the walls that enclose the pit, marking his territory with sprays of urine, and he continually swings his greenish-golden eyes toward the tunnel from which his adversary will soon appear.

* * *

Backstage, still in his cage, Kumal seems nearly comatose. He wants to sleep. The pale man with the honey drop sparked a distant memory, and brought to the tiger for just an instant a warm wash of feelings, but he is reluctant to think back that far. Sleep is less threatening than remembering. But the evil man will not let him rest.

"Come on," Saladin says. "Get a move on, you lazy bastard. You have work to do. You're really going to earn your keep today."

Prodded by Saladin's pitchfork, Kumal drops down from his cage and lumbers toward the tunnel for wild animals that leads directly to the arena. Zerbino's assistants, used to the tiger's recalcitrant ways, bang on metal hoops to force him forward. The slightest shadow of sadness shows on Zerbino's features as he watches Kumal amble through the tunnel. The tiger, trained to jump through hoops of fire and nothing more, does not stand a chance to survive combat; his young life will end before dusk. Saladin broke the young tiger's spirit.

The animal tamer makes a furtive sign of the cross, careful not to be seen by his wife.

"God be with you, my brother," he mumbles under his breath.

* * *

McRory walks away from the arena with Nai-Rea, holding tight to her hand. They move past the sumptuously decorated buffets where servants are waiting to receive guests after the festivities. McRory's face is swollen and raw, and he wipes his nose with a handkerchief soaked in blood.

"I'm finished here," he says. "I have something important to discuss with you."

She looks at him but says nothing.

"If I asked you to come with me—back to my own country—would you consider it?"

With the hint of a tender smile, she says, "You do not ask the statues. Why are you asking me?"

"The statues do not speak to me, but you do. Can't you see that?"

She squeezes his hand. "I'm trying to understand, Aidan." She leans toward him and gently kisses his bruised jawbone.

15

Prowling back and forth in the pit, Sangha hears the sound of the banging on the hoops and immediately stiffens. He backs up slowly, emitting a low, steady growl and takes up a position facing the tunnel. He crouches, his muscles tight, back arched, ready to pounce. As the barred gate is raised, his growls grow deeper. Slowly, one step at a time, Kumal creeps into the fighting pit, his belly nearly dragging on the ground. He is suddenly aware of the huge audience surrounding him in the bleachers. He is used to small groups that gather to see him leap through hoops of fire. He is terrified. His eyes then fasten on the tiger facing him and baring his fangs in a menacing howl. He looks at the tiger uncomprehendingly, his terror growing. All he wants is his cage, his privacy, the balm of sleep.

He watches warily as the tiger takes a step toward him, transfixed by the shiny object around his neck. The tiger's ears are pinned back, his eyes burning holes of concentration. The tiger now paces slowly in a circle around Kumal, eyes riveted on him, never for an instant glancing away. Sangha moves into a crouching position, ready to spring. Kumal retreats. He wants to go back to the tunnel behind him, but the gate is once again barred, blocking his way.

Sangha continues to stalk him, the low growl steady, unremitting. He fakes a charge to provoke Kumal, but seems confused when he fails to respond. Instead, he slithers along the bars, beginning to whimper. When Sangha again tries to provoke him with a lightning fast sweep of his paw and angry spitting sounds, Kumal turns his back and moves away. Sangha continues to track him, and when Kumal is pinned against a corner of the pit he lets out a roar, his ears pinned back, his tail thrashing furiously. He is desperate now, pushed finally beyond the threshold of fear. He is ready to fight.

The tigers face off against each other, their eyes locked in mutual challenge. They come slowly closer and growl, each waiting for the other to make the move that will signal a struggle to the death. But then Kumal suddenly freezes, oblivious to the impatient clapping and catcalls from the stands, oblivious to everything except the tiger no more than a foot away. Kumal's nostrils widen. He sniffs the air, his head cocked to one side. An image flitters through his mind—a temple, a forest. It is a distant image, but troubling.

Sangha lets loose a piercing roar. He is low to the ground, about to attack. But Kumal still does not move. His ears are no longer pinned back in combat mode; instead, they prick up. He blows gently through his lips, producing a strange purring sound. Listening intently now, Sangha retreats a step and his body sways as he stares at Kumal. In his mind's eye he sees a smiling face set in stone. He sees two tiger cubs romping in play near the smiling stone face. His tail goes limp as he stares at the tiger in front of him. Suddenly he makes the same purring sound.

The two tigers rush together. They stand on their hind legs and fall forward into a tight huddle. They begin to paw at each other, growling softly, and roll over on the ground, all tangled up. They bite each other's neck as they cavort on the dusty ground of the fighting pit. Suddenly Sangha stands and turns around, presenting his hindquarters to Kumal, and lets his tail drop under his brother's snout. Kumal, with a soft growl, snatches the tail in his teeth and they do a little dance, crooning as they move.

A collective shiver goes through the spectators. The tiger fight, billed as a bloody battle to the death, has taken a strange turn and no one knows what to make of it. There are scattered catcalls, some stomping of feet and impatient clapping of hands, but for the most part the arena is strangely silent, and the silence grows and spreads from section to section. The audience recognizes that it is witnessing a unique—if perhaps bizarre—demonstration of tiger behavior. Slaughter and blood is now forgotten as the spectators hang on to every movement and gesture and sound of these very strange tigers.

McRory and Nai-Rea, who had reached the exit gate, stop as they react to the lack of sound from the arena.

"What do you suppose is happening?" McRory says.

"I have no idea. Should we go back and see?"

Puzzled, they turn back.

* * *

Kumal and Sangha are no longer aware of the audience that swells the arena or even of the arena itself. They are cubs again, just as they were in the old days when the days were full of play and discovery and there were no dark places in their world. Sangha pulls Kumal along by the tail, and with his claws deployed, he seems to be paddling along. Behind him, Kumal sits on his hindquarters and leaves tracks in the dust of the pit as he sings his purring song.

Catching sight of the golden globe that has rolled into a corner, Kumal suddenly leaps and grabs hold of the ball. With one paw he rolls it to his brother. Sangha blocks it and pushes it back to Kumal. This time Kumal keeps it, and the game takes a new turn. He nudges the ball in circles, with little bursts of speed as he tries to outmaneuver his brother. Emitting a series of high yipping sounds, Sangha leaps forward, wrestles Kumal to the ground and manages to recover the ball.

In the arena the silence begins to shift to excited conversation and even an undercurrent of laughter. The audience is now totally absorbed in this curious spectacle, a form of theater they never expected to see.

Raoul nudges his mother. "Don't you remember, Mama? That's what we used to do. Our own kind of soccer game."

She squeezes his hand, too absorbed in the scene to answer.

Normandin leans close to his wife and whispers, "The gods have cursed me again. His Excellency was expecting a bloody tiger fight, not this comedy."

"Relax, Eugene. There's never been a show like this. If you ask me, the gods are smiling on you. Look over at His Excellency—he seems amused."

McRory is also amused. Having returned, he stands with Nai-Rea near the steps leading to the bleachers. "They're back in the wild," he says, "not a care in the world. What a beautiful sight." He takes Nai-Rea's arm and she rests her head on his shoulder.

"Did you ever see anything like this when you were hunting?"

"I'm afraid I wasn't looking for it. I had only one thing on my mind."

Although His Excellency seems absorbed in the frolicking of the tigers, a shadow passes over the face of the majordomo. What would His Excellency's father have thought of this travesty? He makes a sign and members of the royal staff storm into the arena and up to the pit, armed with pitchforks and pickaxes; Saladin and his assistants are not far behind them. They all try to poke the tigers through the bars, hoping to rouse the warrior spirit in them.

The two tigers stop playing. They leap to their feet and roar. Side by side they face off against these hated upright creatures, ready to attack. Hurling profanities at the tigers, Saladin rushes at Kumal and stabs at him with a pitchfork. Snarling with rage, Sangha grabs Saladin's arm in his jaws, pulling the suddenly terrified magician toward him. Saladin struggles against the Herculean strength of the tiger, screaming at the top of his lungs. Sangha drags him up against the bars of the pit, and in spite of the narrow passage he pulls him partway through the bars. Kumal watches, his head cocked to one side. He has a distant memory of his father, the Great Tiger, confronting an upright creature, then the popping sound and the flash of light and his father sprawled on the ground. Kumal is afraid for his brother.

The laughter in the arena has vanished, and in its place are boos and cries of horror. Many spectators are rushing for the aisles.

Zerbino opens the gate to the fighting pit and eases himself inside. He raises his rifle and takes aim at Sangha. With a roar, Kumal rears up at the animal tamer just at the instant he fires. The familiar explosion rings out (the sound Kumal remembers—the one that changed his life), but he no longer fears it. He slams Zerbino to the ground with one swift swipe of his paw. Sangha moves swiftly to the door of the fighting pit, which was left ajar in the confusion. He steps over Saladin, stuck between the bars, unconscious and badly mauled, and is suddenly outside in the expanse of the arena. Kumal drops his prey and quickly follows his brother.

Screams ring out. Chaos reigns. Dignitaries, bureaucrats, local landowners and their wives break into a panic-stricken stampede.

Normandin grabs Raoul, who is resisting.

"I want to go to him," the boy wails. "He's my tiger. I want to go to Sangha. They're going to kill him."

"And a good thing, too," Normandin says, pulling his son along roughly by the arm. "He's already a man-killer. You just saw the evidence."

"They prodded him with pitchforks," Raoul shouts. "What do you expect him to do?"

"You're insolent," his father hisses at him. "You'll hear about this later, young man."

In the confusion, His Excellency's servants rush to take hold of his gilded chair. Studying the set expression on the youthful potentate's face, Normandin sees his world collapsing around him. He pulls the papers out of his briefcase and rushes forward.

"Your Excellency, wait. Please wait!"

But he is too late. The servants have lifted the chair and are hurrying it away, pushing people to the left and right, clearing a path. Looking back over his shoulder with a mocking smile of helplessness, His Excellency shrugs and spreads his hands, palms upward, as though to say, "What do you expect me to do? This is out of my hands."

As Normandin turns back, he is caught in the crush of the panicking crowd moving for the exits with the single-minded force of a stampede of buffalo. Someone jostles him hard and the papers still clutched in his hand fly everywhere. With a bleat of dismay, he tries to retrieve them but they are trampled underfoot. He spots McRory in the crowd and bulls his way toward him, tears of frustration in his eyes.

"McRory—please! The tigers....We need your help!"

The hunter regards him coldly. "I'm through playing your games, Normandin. I'm sorry, but this time you're on your own. Keep the statues. Put me in prison, if you must. I want nothing more to do with any of this."

"But the animals," he pleads. "They're running wild. What am I going to do?"

"That, Monsieur l'Administrateur," McRory says, "is between you and the tigers."

16

Outside of the arena, a kilted musician, his bagpipes slung over his shoulders, is scouting the area nervously. All anyone can think about now, the village obsession, is the threat of two tigers on the loose, man-eating tigers. Rifles that haven't seen use for years are dusted off, oiled and loaded.

Behind the intrepid, kilted musician, His Excellency's band anxiously awaits his report. The musician peeks around the corner of a building, quickly pulls back and takes off running at full speed, followed by the rest of the band. Around the corner of the building, Kumal and Sangha appear at no more than a walk, apparently not in pursuit of anyone. Kumal stops suddenly. He sees his cage on the animal tamer's truck. By force of habit, he leaps up through the open door. Sangha keeps walking toward the trees adjoining the grounds, then he stops and turns around, head tilted to one side, and stares at his brother who is lying down in a corner of the cage. He advances toward the cage and watches as Kumal curls up snugly, rests his chin on his crossed paws and closes his eyes.

A growling starts deep in Sangha's throat and slowly builds in intensity. Kumal opens his eyes a little and sees Sangha, after one final roar, heading away from His Excellency's estate. Kumal stands up and shakes his entire body. He hesitates a moment before walking cautiously to the open cage door. Another moment of indecision and then he jumps down and runs to catch up with his brother.

The two tigers stroll away through the French gardens, trampling on the buttercup beds and ravaging the delicate clumps of forget-me-nots and begonias. They approach the tall trees adjoining the grounds, the tops of which are tinged red in the setting sun. These images are familiar to the two brothers, pieces of their past, and they feel a great weight lift from their hearts.

As they continue to walk, an old bus clatters over a trail on a hillside. The two tigers, on the high ground, see a whole stock of goats, chickens and ducks packed on the roof of the bus. At the wheel, the driver hears a heavy thud over his head. An instant later, stricken with terror, he sees a tiger tail on the windshield, swishing back and forth like a single furry wiper.

"What the hell is *that*?" the man exclaims. The bus swerves, goes off into a ditch and into the trunk of a coconut tree. Sangha and Kumal climb inside the bus and begin ripping apart the seats. Sangha tears open a suitcase in the netting over his head with his claws. He sits on the horn (the driver having abandoned the bus) and makes it beep. They ignore the passengers as though they are upright creatures of no consequence. The trembling, terrified passengers pile out of the bus and take to the roadside and to trees with branches low enough to climb where they wait for the end of the carnage on their bus. On one of the higher branches, the driver clutches a pouch to his chest containing the day's receipts.

Kumal and Sangha soon lose interest in the bus and move on. In the European quarter they come to a house with the front door left slightly ajar. They bound up the porch steps and into the front parlor. Kumal climbs the stairs to the second floor, sniffing the air and smelling something deliciously sweet. He enters a room cloudy with steam and redolent of perfume. He stares at the large white bathtub and then his glance lingers on the woman in the tub screaming at the top of her lungs. Her screaming makes him nervous and he backs away as she bolts from the tub, streaming water, and flies past the surprised tiger, down the stairs and out of the house.

The bathtub continues to draw his attention. He approaches it carefully, as though it might be some new form of living creature. When he's satisfied that it isn't alive, he leaps over the edge and dives into the soapy water. He emerges, making gurgling sounds and smothered in bubbles. Sangha has joined his brother in the bathroom and is busy ransacking the medicine cabinet. He squashes a tube of pink toothpaste and gives a growl of surprise as it squirts in his face and stings his eyes.

When the bathroom begins to lose its charm, the two brothers invade the kitchen. Kumal forces his paw underneath the hinge that holds the icebox closed and sniffs the delicious aromas inside. With a yelp of delight, he proceeds to knock the contents from the shelves onto the floor and laps up a pool of spilt milk.

Above him, Sangha is swinging from the light fixture in the ceiling. After devouring a cold slice of pork, along with part of the paper it was wrapped in, Kumal grabs his brother's tail. Under the weight of the two tigers, the ceiling caves in.

Again it is time to move on.

* * *

For the next few days the brothers live a charmed and carefree life. Posses are out to capture or kill them, but they elude them all, and while doing so, manage to terrorize the village and other nearby communities without causing harm to anyone. The day following their escape a newspaper headline proclaims: TERROR AT THE PALACE. ONE VICTIM SAVAGED, DOZENS TRAMPLED IN THE PANIC. The black-and-white photograph shows the limp body of Saladin stuck in the bars, and an insert features the heads of the two tigers looking particularly murderous, with bared fangs and wild eyes.

The siege of the tigers takes many curious turns. On their second day of freedom, Sangha nudges his way into a newspaper kiosk, and when a passerby strolls over to the newsstand to purchase a paper, he discovers Sangha in place of the newsman, paws up on the counter. The man is so dumbfounded that he picks up a paper, drops his money on the counter and calmly walks away. Once he turns the corner, out of view of the tiger, he runs for his life.

On their third day of freedom, the two tigers encounter an official procession making its way solemnly across a bamboo bridge that spans a shallow river. When the two brothers suddenly appear from the opposite end of the bridge, the native secretaries in their black robes come to a stunned halt. Then they scurry away in all directions, their arms held high as though they are thieves confronting a policeman holding a pistol. Some turn tail and run, others jump into the river with their umbrellas and briefcases. Behind the group in front, four carriers set down a palanquin, and a dignitary, wearing a top hat, peers through the window, wondering what the fuss is all about. When he sees two tigers advancing nonchalantly toward him, he hurriedly steps down from the palanquin. Backing up, speechless with shock, and clutching a fishbowl to his chest inside of which is Administrator Normandin's large goldfish, the dignitary loses his footing when his oversized sandal gets caught between two pieces of bamboo. With a cry of distress he falls over the low bridge railing into the river, still holding tight to the fishbowl. As the dignitary paddles clumsily to shore, the goldfish swims away in the shallow water.

Kumal and Sangha, heedless to the danger that surrounds them, are reveling in the joy of reunion. Their bodies may have grown large, they may have the look of ferocious beasts, but in their hearts they are cubs again, carefree and playful. No longer confined to cages, they are once again sharing new experiences.

As they move through the countryside, a track marked UPPER MEKONG BUTCHERS, which is transporting a large steer carcass into town, passes them. Their nostrils are immediately on the alert. The smells that waft from the truck are unbearably appetizing, and without so much as a glance at each other, their minds are as one. They take off in hot pursuit of the truck. The driver glances frantically in the rearview mirror and floors the gas pedal, but even when the speedometer can't climb any higher, the tigers are still gaining on him. The driver, his bull neck swollen even thicker with fear, tries ramming the wheel to the left and right, hoping this tactic will thwart the tigers. But the smell is thick in the air and the tigers are not to be denied.

Suddenly he can no longer see his pursuers; they seem to have simply vanished. As he nears the top of an incline, he breathes a sigh of relief. The truck is racing downhill now and those beasts, wherever they are, will never catch him. The butcher keeps checking the rearview mirror, and he wipes his brow, sighing deeply. What the butcher cannot see, though, is the deepest recess of the carrier, closest to the rear window. That is where Kumal and Sangha have quickly separated the steer carcass from one of its legs and are happily feasting on the choice cut of beef—one of the most delicious meals of their young lives.

Later that day, lazy with full stomachs, they lie on top of a pile of logs taking their siesta. But Kumal cannot remain still for long; adventure nags at him and exerts its pull. Soon he is leaping from one tree stump to another, sitting up and extending his paw as if on his circus stool, running through his repertoire of tricks taught him by Zerbino. Sangha follows his brother's strange antics and moves his head from side to side as though following a tennis match. But he soon grows bored. His mouth widens in an impressive yawn.

Suddenly shots ring out. Bullets strike the logs under Sangha, sending wood chips flying. Both tigers scamper away as the firing intensifies.

17

By the end of the week, the village looks like an entrenched camp, ready for war. The two tigers have been sighted many times, but they seem to be leading a charmed life. They have been shot at repeatedly, but even the most skilled among the village's marksmen haven't been able to bring them down. As protection against these marauding beasts, fires have been lit around the edges of the village. The frightened village people crowd around the native soldiers who are standing guard, their rifles aimed at the forest beyond.

The guards at the forward perimeter turn their heads at the sound of a motor and watch as a military truck jolts up and stops in the square. There is scattered applause as McRory emerges from the truck, rifle in hand. Nai-Rea follows behind him. The villagers consider the great hunter their savior; they are confident that he can rid the countryside of those beasts if anyone can. Cheers arise to join the hand clapping, but McRory, staring straight ahead and looking grave, does not respond.

Normandin descends the steps of the chief's hut and pushes his way through the crowd, accompanied by the old chief and his son, the crippled boy. He warmly shakes McRory's hand.

"I wasn't sure you'd come," he says.

"Nor was I, actually." He glances at Nai-Rea. "But I was told I was thinking selfishly and shirking my duty. So here I am."

"Thank you. We are most grateful. This is a dreadful situation."

"Where are the tigers now? Have they been spotted?"

"They're not far," Normandin answers. "My soldiers got some good shots at them at a lumber camp in the forest. But they managed to slip away."

"Shots that miss are not good shots," McRory says. "They are almost as bad as shots that wound but don't kill."

His gaze falls on Raoul Normandin who has appeared above the veranda. The Administrator follows his gaze and shakes his head. "We had to tell him that we gave his tiger to His Excellency. He didn't take it very well. He thought we'd sent him to a zoo in Saigon."

"So you lied to him."

"We thought it best, under the circumstances. Many of His Excellency's beasts are bred for combat. His forebears had been doing that for many generations." The Administrator clears his throat nervously. "My son wouldn't have approved."

"I can understand that," McRory says. "Why are you telling me this?"

"I don't suppose you'd speak to him. I would be terribly grateful."

"How do you know I'll say what you want me to say?"

"I have to trust you, McRory. I have no choice."

Some distance away, in her father's hut, Nai-Rea is crouching before the small shrine of her ancestors. She silently arranges sticks of incense and offerings, but her full attention is on the words of McRory, which reach her, slightly muffled, from the outside. Like the Administrator, she is praying that McRory will say the right things to the boy; that he will find a way to explain the pitfalls of sentimentalizing the kingdom of beasts, which is far from the peaceable kingdom featured in children's books.

In the light of an oil lamp, McRory and Raoul move to a corner of the veranda that affords them privacy. They sit cross-legged, facing each other. Night has fallen and the sky is filled with stars. McRory sips tea as he searches for the right words.

Finally he says, "You see that old man over there leaning on his cane and that woman with her child? And what about that boy. He must be about your age."

Raoul nods. "I see them." He says nothing more, waiting for the hunter to continue.

"What would you say if you found out tomorrow that your tiger had torn off their legs or eaten them. What would you feel then?"

"Sangha would never eat anyone, and—and—I think my father put you up to this."

"I'm not here because of your father. It's for the people of this village—I agreed to come to help them, and I'm talking to you because I want to. Your father has nothing to do with it."

"Sangha is not a killer," the boy says.

"But he will be, Raoul. And it won't be long before it happens."

"If he wanted to, he would've already done it."

"Let me tell you about the jungle," McRory says. "It happens to be something I know about. Sangha has never learned the laws of the jungle, and they are essential for survival. He would have learned them from his parents, but he was separated from them at too young an age. Worse, he's not afraid of humans. Deer will be too fast for him. He doesn't have the art of stalking and cornering game. That leaves him few options when the hunger pangs grow sharp and drive him. He'll go for the easiest prey then—the women in the fields, the children….All animals that escape from captivity are man-eaters when they return to the wild. They have no other choice."

As he listens, Raoul's eyes harden with distrust.

"But Sangha is not like that. I know he isn't. Our dog Bitzy went after him again and again until Sangha was forced to fight back. He was only protecting himself."

"The point is, Raoul, he did fight back. And when they do it, it's usually fatal."

174

"I'm telling you, Sangha is no killer."

"You *hope* he isn't. But he is—it's built into his nature."

The boy stares hard at the hunter. "Are you saying you don't love Kumal?"

"Yes, I love him. More than you know."

Raoul blows his nose and says brusquely, "Then I don't see how you can kill them. You don't kill what you love."

"If I don't do the job someone else will."

In the corner near her small shrine, Nai-Rae closes her eyes, joins her hands and begins to pray. She prays for the boy, for McRory, for decisions so painfully difficult to make.

The boy and the man are silent for a moment. Beyond the veranda the jungle rustles with its mysterious hidden life.

"Raoul," McRory says after a reflective pause, "I took Kumal from the jungle. I let you keep Sangha. These were not wise decisions on my part, and this whole tragedy is my fault. It's up to me to end it."

McRory says this matter-of-factly, without a trace of self-pity. He glances at Nai-Rae and continues. "Someone once told me—someone very wise—to leave things as they are in the jungle. He was right. I decided to meddle and it was a mistake. I also meddled in another way, by hunting for profit, not as a means of survival—and that's also wrong. When this is over, I swear I'll never touch a rifle again. I'll leave the statues and the tigers in peace. I'll go back to my country. And when I get there I'll marry the woman I love and live in peace, writing books."

"Then go write them now," Raoul says, unmoved by his words.

"I can't. There's unfinished business to tend to."

The boy shakes his head stubbornly. "Sangha isn't a killer, and nothing you say will convince me. Kumal isn't either. They'll stay in the jungle. They'll learn to hunt. They're not too old to learn."

"Who will teach them, Raoul?"

The boy is silent, his face set in defiance. He is still unconvinced.

* * *

Hours later, the two tigers slip out of the bush and approach the bridge of eighteen Buddhas. In the misty light of dawn the busts appear like a gathering of ghosts. Kumal and Sangha sniff the air and carefully inventory the area. Reassured, Kumal enters the bridge (once again assuming the leadership position as he did when they were cubs), Sangha following at his heels. Across the bridge and at the top of a high hill, the forest stretches across numerous ridges as far as the eye can see, and arising from the vast sea of vegetation are the towers of the overgrown temple where they were born. The tigers stare down the incline, bathed in the strengthening light of dawn. Camouflaged by brush, they watch as two military trucks come to a stop in the

176

clearing. McRory, carrying his rifle angled across his waist, and the chief, clutching his bugle, step down from the cabin of the lead truck. Behind them, soldiers jump to the ground and help the villagers unload dozens of gas cans. In a column, carrying the gas cans on their heads, the soldiers walk off into the jungle.

War has been declared. The battle against the two young tigers has been joined.

Kumal and Sangha, on the valley floor now, keep moving toward the temple. When the sound of a bugle rips through the silence, the two tigers come to a stop, their ears pinned back. As the sound of the bugle call grows louder, they take off in the opposite direction. Seconds later a loud explosion rings out, rolling like thunder from hillside to hillside. The ground trembles beneath their running feet. A cloud of black smoke darkens the sky and the cloud rides the wind and races in their direction. For a moment the tigers hesitate, uncertain of the safest course to take, and when Sangha sees Kumal start to double back toward the hill they had just traversed, he follows after his brother.

At the edge of a field of tall grass, a soldier strikes a match and the grass explodes in a huge ball of flame. Other soldiers pour the contents of their gas cans onto the brush, and, ignited, a wall of fire is formed, closing in the entire valley. Starting at the top of the hill and working downward, the hungry flames devour the brush, rumbling with fury, and moving at the speed of a galloping horse. When the flames race toward Kumal and Sangha, they again make an about-face and hurtle down from rock to rock. On the valley floor, they run into a second wall of flame, barring their passage. Kumal and Sangha are surrounded. They flee in the only direction not entirely consumed by flames—the direction that leads to the gorge where the soldiers are waiting with rifles poised.

McRory shades his eyes from the sun and picks up his binoculars, swinging them around in a slow arc until he spots the two tigers in the distance—small swift-moving creatures emerging from the cloud of smoke and running straight toward the gorge.

"Get ready," McRory shouts.

The soldiers grab their rifles and rest them tight against their shoulders, waiting for the hunter's command. When the first shots are fired, Sangha stops short. He has seen the flashes behind the smoke and his instinct tells him that the flashes may pose a danger even greater than the fire. He growls and works his body close to the ground. There is another series of flashes, which cause Kumal to stop as well. Behind them the fire is quickly advancing, devouring everything in its path. They can feel its scalding breath. The tigers stand together, undecided. Wafts of smoke and swirling ash sting their eyes and burn their lungs. Sangha turns to Kumal, who looks back and forth between the approaching flames and the line of soldiers in the rocks, rifles aimed at them and firing. While waiting for his brother to make a move, Sangha laps water from the miniscule stream that runs along the bottom of the valley. His throat is parched and his eyes blurred from the smoke. He begins to whimper. Kumal turns from him and faces the fire. Slowly, he approaches the inferno. The flames reflect in his pupils, his muscles ripple in anticipation. His ears are pinned to his head.

He jumps.

In a single bound, he disappears through the wall of flames, memories of the evil creatures and their hoop of fire swirling in his head. He is now on the other side of the wall of fire, in a desolate landscape of smoke and ash. His coat smolders and he shakes his body to rid himself of the pain.

He stands as close as he can to the edge of the fire and calls out.

"*Ah-oom! Ah-oom!*"

From the other side of the wall of flame, Sangha answers.

"*Ah-oom! Ah-oom!*"

Sangha paces back and forth before the columns of fire, helpless and desperate as though the red columns are the bars of a cage imprisoning him. He doesn't know what to do. He isn't his brother. He cannot bring himself to advance into the horrible heat and terrifying brilliance of the fire. He knows that he's trapped within his fears.

Suddenly Kumal returns, vaulting high through the flames. He is covered in ash, the plume of his tail singed and smoking. He walks up to Sangha and speaks to him in deep purring sounds. He rubs his head against his brother, and the message is clear: you must trust me, you must come with me into the fire. There is no other way.

McRory, half hidden in the swirling smoke, watches the two tigers through the binoculars. They are standing still, face to face, as if absorbed in a silent conversation.

"Why does it have to come to this?" he mutters under his breath. "Why?"

As he watches, Kumal turns around and faces the fire. He lowers his body and once again takes a running jump through the flames. Sangha hesitates; he turns around in a circle several times.

"Come on," McRory mutters, his binoculars glued to his eyes. "You can do it! You can do it!"

Finally the young tiger coils up and leaps through the flames after his brother.

McRory lowers his binoculars and a slow smile spreads across his face.

* * *

In the shade of a canvas spread between two trucks, Normandin rereads a portion of a letter he has been struggling to write.

"Your Excellency:

"I am most sorry to learn that my government has decided to abandon the temple road project just at the

180

moment when I can promise you that the two animals responsible for the disturbance have been destroyed. The benefits which will accrue to this country from the road into the jungle...." Normandin breaks off with a sudden pang of apprehension. His son was sitting across from him only seconds ago and now he is nowhere to be seen.

"Raoul?" he calls out as he labors to his feet. "Raoul—*where are you?*"

No answer. He scans the deserted clearing where the trucks are parked, his jowls jiggling with agitation.

"Raoul?" he calls out again. His voice trembles and a pain knifes through his chest.

He hears the crackling of branches and McRory appears, sweating profusely.

"It's Raoul," the Administrator says, slumping into his seat again. "He's gone. My God...if anything has happened...I mean, my wife, Mathilde. How could I ever face her again."

"I'll go look for him," McRory says. "You stay here in case he returns."

* * *

At the bottom of a wooded slope, the two tigers are leaping around in the clear water of a stream, cleaning the ash and smoke from their coats and soothing the burns they've sustained. A noise startles Sangha and he stands in the water and lets out a low, menacing growl.

181

As the tigers look toward the source of the sound, they see a small boy emerging from the bushes.

He calls out softly, "Sangha? Sangha?"

Kumal's ears prick up. He growls and starts to move forward, but his brother stops growling and walks in front of him.

"Sangha," the boy repeats. "It's Raoul. I've come to find you. I know you're here somewhere."

The tiger emerges from the stream and walks up to the child.

Raoul grins. He pets the tiger and kisses him on the snout. "I hoped you'd recognize me. You haven't been gone that long." He leans over and whispers in the tiger's ear, "You must never come back to the village of men. Do you hear me? Never. Promise me you won't. You must stay in the jungle forever."

Lying down a short distance away, observing his brother and the boy intently, Kumal suddenly turns his head. Something is moving in the tall grass. He sits up and growls deep in his chest. McRory moves with the stealth of a practiced hunter, and in his sights is the head of the tiger standing next to Normandin's son. He watches as the boy whispers in the tiger's ear, then removes the necklace from around his neck. He throws it away in the bush.

Slowly McRory's finger relaxes on the trigger. He then hears breathing right next to him, and, whirling around, he discovers a pair of greenish-golden eyes regarding him not five feet away.

The hunter and the tiger study each other for a moment and then Kumal comes closer. McRory forces himself to remain motionless. The tiger's snout dips toward McRory's hand, and, nostrils flared, he starts to sniff it. Slowly, without any abrupt movements, McRory takes his weapon from his shoulder and lays it on the ground. He then searches in his pockets but there are no more honey drops.

With an apologetic smile he shows Kumal his empty palm. "Forgive me," he says. "I ate the last one this morning. If I'd only known…"

He drops his eyes to his rifle, but then lifts them again. The hunter and the tiger continue to look at each other, completely motionless.

McRory puts out a hand and rubs the tiger's neck. At his touch, Kumal's back arches and he moves closer to the man.

"Goodbye, Kumal," McRory says. "It's time for you to return to the jungle."

As Sangha moves away along the trail that winds through the forest, Kumal joins him. At the edge of the line of trees, Sangha turns and stares at the boy and the man standing beside him.

"*Aaroom! Aaroom!*"

His bellow echoes in the forest.

Kumal, standing beside his brother, then delivers the same powerful sound.

"*Aaroom!*"

McRory listens intently as he leans on his rifle. After a moment's silence there is an answering roar in the distance.

"*Aaroom! Aaroom!*"

McRory turns to Raoul, a smile lighting his features. "Did you hear that? Another tiger is answering them."

Raoul nods, his eyes red. He is struggling not to cry.

"The animal must know them," McRory says. "Tigers have the ability to sort through sounds and identify them."

"Maybe this tiger can teach them to hunt," Raoul says hopefully.

"Let's hope so."

McRory puts his arm around the boy's shoulder.

"Are you all right?" he says.

"I'm all right. But I'm going to miss Sangha."

"What will you tell them in the village, Raoul? We have to have a story. The same one."

"I'll tell them what I saw. That they disappeared in the flames." He looks up at McRory. "Nothing could survive that—right?"

"I don't see how."

McRory watches the forest for a moment, his keen hunter's eye searching for the tigers' movements. Then he turns back to the boy.

"We're taking a big chance, you know."

Raoul nods slowly. "I know. But that's good, isn't it? To take a chance sometimes?"

184

"Yes," McRory answers. "Sometimes it is good, and today it feels very good indeed."

They stare for a long while at the place where the two tigers entered the dark and hidden forest of thick, overarching trees, their sanctuary from the world of upright creatures. But they are gone. The boy cries silently and the hunter pretends not to notice.

*   *   *

It is early evening of the same day and the setting sun reflects on a moss-covered, bas-relief sculpture. Kumal and Sangha advance slowly over the loose paving stones of the terrace. They scan the mass of ferns in front of them; they growl, their ears pinned flat against their necks. As they watch, there is a shiver in the ferns, which slowly part, and a third tiger emerges and slowly approaches them.

The three tigers set out on the path, sculpted with sacred images, that leads to the riverbank. All three enter the calm waters, bathe for a few moments, all three making low purring sounds, and then on shore they stretch out in a remaining patch of light. Kumal and Sangha study the third tiger and see the traces of an old head wound. There is a hole through the bottom of her left ear.

Kumal and Sangha lie close to her. They rest their heads against the flanks of the Tigress. They lick her fur and breathe in her familiar odor. She licks them in turn.

185

Nearby, under the foliage, the shimmering water illuminates the pink sandstone face of an ancient Buddha. On his lips is a smile of eternal benevolence.

Producer, director, and co-writer **Jean-Jacques Annaud** most recently directed *Enemy at the Gates.* Annaud's debut feature, *Black and White in Color/La Victoire En Chatant,* won the Academy Award® in 1977 for Best Foreign Language Film. His next feature was *Coup de Tête,* a great success in Europe, followed by *Quest for Fire,* which earned him a César Award as Best Director. Next, he directed *The Name of the Rose,* which received a César Award for Best Foreign Film. Annaud also co-wrote screenplays for the latter two films with Alain Godard. In 1989, Annaud received international acclaim and another César Award for *The Bear.* Annaud's other films include *The Lover, Wings of Courage,* the first feature film made in IMAX-3D; and *Seven Years in Tibet.*

Novelist **James Whitfield Ellison** is the author of seven novels and ten novelizations of major motion pictures. He lives in New York City.

Ask for these titles at your local bookstore, or order from: Newmarket Press, 18 East 48th Street, New York, NY 10017, (212) 832-3575 or (800) 669-3903.

JAMES OLIVER CURWOOD NATURE TRILOGY

The Bear (Originally published as *The Grizzly King)*

The spectacular success of the movie triggered the rediscovery of this long-lost adventure story about Thor, a mighty grizzly, and Muskwa, a motherless bear cub, who travel from one adventure to another while trappers draw nearer and nearer. "Spellbinding—as thrilling as the movie." —*The Kirkus Reviews* (208 pages; digest paperback)

Kazan, Father of Baree

The first book in Curwood's nature series, this is the thrilling and truly unforgettable story of Kazan, three-quarters dog and one-quarter wolf, the mightiest canine of the Canadian wilderness. (240 pages; digest paperback)

Baree, The Story of a Wolf-Dog

The third book in Curwood's nature trilogy is a powerful adventure story about a half-wild wolf pup separated from his parents in the Canadian wilderness, and the otters, rabbits, owls, bears, and other creatures he encounters there. "A timeless tale... Curwood captures the simplicity and beauty of nature." —*ALA Booklist* (256 pages; digest paperback)

Finding Forrester
A Novel by James W. Ellison
Based on the screenplay written by Mike Rich

When Jamal—a talented African-American scholar-athlete who is recruited by an elite Manhattan prep school for his brilliance on and off the basketball court—sneaks into the apartment of Forrester, the neighborhood recluse, he accidentally leaves behind his backpack full of writings, and they both get something unexpected in return. "A polished and compelling young adult book." — *The New York Times* (192 pages; digest paperback)

Fly Away Home
A Novel by Patricia Hermes
Based on the screenplay written by Robert Rodat and Vince McKewin

After Amy Alden discovers a nest of goose eggs and brings them home to hatch, the newborns follow her everywhere, claiming her as their mother. As they grow, Amy and her dad Thomas realize they must take on the responsibility of teaching the geese how to migrate for the winter. Includes a 16-page section on the making of the film. (160 pages; digest paperback)

Spider Riders: The Shards of the Oracle
Tedd Anasti and Patsy Cameron-Anasti
with Stephen D. Sullivan

The adventurous tale of Hunter Steele, a 13-year-old boy who chases a spider into a mysterious cave and discovers the kingdom of Arachnia. Unable to return home, he must prove himself worth of wearing the special manacle of a Spider Rider. But first he must catch his own battle spider and master mind talk in order to communicate with him. (224 pages; digest paperback)

Two Brothers: The Tale of Kumal and Sangha
A Novel by James Ellison
Based on the motion picture screenplay written by
Alain Godard & Jean-Jacques Annaud

Deep in the heart of the Southeast Asian jungle, two tigers are born in the ruins of a forgotten temple. Fortune hunters searching the jungle for ancient treasure penetrate the tigers' sanctuary—separating them from each other and their parents. When they are grown and reunited, Kumal and Sangha will face their greatest challenge yet. (192 pages; digest paperback)